At the Rising of the Moon: Irish Stories and Studies

Frank James Mathew

AT THE RISING OF THE MOON

"AT THE RISING OF THE MOON."

AT THE RISING OF
THE MOON

IRISH STORIES AND STUDIES

BY

FRANK MATHEW

ILLUSTRATIONS BY FRED PEGRAM
AND
A. S. BOYD

LONDON
McCLURE & CO.
33 BEDFORD STREET, COVENT GARDEN
SIMPKIN, MARSHALL, HAMILTON, KENT & CO., LTD.
STATIONERS' HALL COURT, E.C.
1893

To

MY FRIEND

JEROME K. JEROME

CONTENTS

x CONTENTS

LIST OF ILLUSTRATIONS

PROLOGUE

SHAMROCKS

As I was lately turning over some dusty papers here in my chambers in the Temple, I came on a dried weed. At first I wondered how it got here, and then saw that it was a bit of shamrock, and remembered gathering it—years ago now—on a moor by Liscannor. At the sight of it my thoughts went back to old times on the West Coast of Ireland, and to many friends of mine there—landlords, moonlighters and others; and then I resolved to write out these stories, for fear that some day I should find my memory of my friends as faded as the shamrocks.

AT THE RISING OF THE MOON

THE REVEREND PETER FLANNERY

"HE SANG IN HIS TURN"

My friend the Reverend Peter Flannery is the sternest looking and the gentlest of men. To look at him you would fancy he had spent a fierce life; but the truth is that he has lived in a wilderness and that in his broad parish of Moher there is not a mouse afraid of him.

I first met him in an hotel at

A

Lisdoonvarna. One night there was singing, and a big, truculent old priest sang in his turn:

> "When we went a-gipsying,
>   A long time ago."

He was very serious and hoarse. With his grim face and white hair he looked the last man in the world to "go a-gipsying." Afterwards I came to know Peter, and spent many evenings with him in the little house where he lives with an old housekeeper of singular ugliness and a turbulent small boy known as Patrick Flannery. I found him absurdly simple, a man knowing nothing of the world and troubling himself little about anything beyond the borders of Moher; but though he is so unpretending he has deep respect for his dignity as a parish-priest.

On one of those evenings in his naked little parlour he told me the story of the only adventure of his life.

A small island with a ruined house on it lies near the shore of the most desolate part of the parish; at high tide it is ringed with white jumping waves but at ebb it is set in a black rim of rocks. A miser was strangled there for his money by his daughter, seventy years ago, so the house is known for miles around as the " House of the Murder." Then it was a headland, but afterwards the encroaching sea cut it off from the coast. The Moher folk say the island is haunted by the ghost of an old man with a choked face and with purple foam on his lips, and is given up to the Evil Spirits.

One stormy winter's night, nearly twelve years ago now, Peter Flannery was riding back from visiting a dying woman near Liscannor. It was raining, the wind was dead against him; he had seldom been out on such a night though his life-work took him on many a wild lonely ride. As he reached the Liscannor Cross-roads his horse stopped, and a heart-broken voice came from under the trees:

"Remember the Dark Man! For God's sake remember the Dark Man!"

He knew that it was Andy Lonergan, the "Dark Man"—that is, the blind man—who haunted that place day and night.

"Is that yourself, Andy?" said he.

"'Tis so, your reverence, but 'tis the black night to be abroad, sure the Banshee is keenin' on th' island."

"The Banshee, is it? I know, I know, and manny's the time I've heard that same, Andy. There's never a rough night without her."

"Is it the wind ye mane, father? I know the wind's cry if annyone, but 'twasn't only that on th' island to-night; 'twas a woman's voice, sometimes 'twas like a child's. There'll be sore hearts in Moher the morn."

"Ah well, Andy! manny's the queer thing ye've heard in your time," said Peter, and he rode homewards, but Andy's words kept in his head. Now, the blind man was half crazed, yet dared not lie about the Banshee; perhaps there was some poor soul in trouble out on the island. At last he turned his horse; as he rode back past the Cross-roads he called out, "Are ye there, Andy?" but no answer came. The horse seemed to have strong objections to going seaward, and Peter himself had misgivings; he is a Clare man, the son of a Ballyvaughan fisherman, and though of course he does not believe in the Banshee, yet would rather not have gone where there was any chance of meeting her. Then he thought—suppose Andy was fooling him! He could fancy the blind man sitting hidden and grinning at him as he rode back past the Cross-roads. It would be a fine joke in Moher; he flushed at such irreverence.

Then he reached the shore, and dismounting fastened his horse to a wall, and walked down across the slipping shingle, crunching it under foot; he was tripped by tangles of seaweed, and stumbled over a fishing coracle, could see scarcely a yard in front of him. "'Tis a blind man's holiday," he thought.

" Faith, Dark Andy could see as much as I can, and
why couldn't McCaura leave his coracle in a sensible
place ? " He went to the water's edge, the foam
splashed over him, he could see nothing but the
white flashes of breakers and was deafened by the
noise. A few minutes of this was enough ; he turned
back with a smile at the absurdity of his going out
there at that time of night. " There's no fool like
an old one," he said ; then stopped to listen again,
and in a pause (when the wind seemed to be taking
breath for a howl) heard a child's cry from the
island. How could a baby be on the island in a
hurricane, when there was not a soul for miles around
would go there for love or money at any time ? His
misgivings rushed back with uncanny legends of lost
souls bound on the winds or imprisoned in the waves
that always keep racing towards the land yet always
break before reaching it. This might be some Devil's
trap. True, he could exorcise the Devil, but would
rather not.

He waited during the new howl of the wind—it
seemed endless—then in the next pause heard the
child's voice again, it was an unmistakably human
squall. " 'Tis a child, sure enough," he said, " an' a
strong one at that." The question for him was not
how did the baby get on the island, but how was he
to get it off ? McCaura's cabin was a mile away

across the bog, and on such a night no one would be out except Dark Andy, who would be worse than useless. The only thing was to go out to the island himself, so he groped his way to the coracle.

Now a coracle is a sort of punt, a shallow frame covered with tarpaulin, a ticklish craft, but it can live in the wildest sea, though as Peter said—" 'Tis always on the look-out for a chance to drown ye." He shouldered it as one to the manner born. Many a day and night had he spent afloat in the time when he was a fisher-boy; he thought how often since then he had longed to put out to sea, only his mighty dignity as a parish-priest forbade it. His old bones were stiff, but he was as strong as ever.

Well, to cut a long story short, he launched that coracle and reached the island, not without risky and hard work. Dragging the coracle ashore, he made his way to the ruined house; the roof had fallen in, the windows were gone, only the walls were left. He could see nothing, but the child's cry guided him and then in a corner he found a woman lying huddled on a heap of fallen plaster and laths; her face was to the wall, her left arm clutched a tiny baby. He knelt down by her and touched her forehead—she was dead. By her dress he knew she came from the Arran Islands. Perhaps she had been been brought to the " House of the Murder " to keep

the birth secret; or perhaps the fishers bringing her
to the mainland had been caught by the gale, and
could place her in no better shelter in the time of her
trouble. Now the Arran folk were familiar to him,
many were of his kindred; he must have known this
woman from her babyhood, and as a slip of a girl
running barefoot on the hills. He turned her face
to him, but could only see it dimly; it was much
changed too, and half hidden by wet hair. Then
the thought came that he had no right to pry into
her secret; he laid her head back reverently. She
lay there with her face to the wall as if she had died
in shame.

He took the baby and chafed it, wrapping his woollen
comforter round it; he thought it was dying—his
knowledge of babies was small—so he decided to
baptise it at once. There was no lack of water for
the rain was still falling in torrents, so he filled a cup
that was lying with some untasted food by the
mother, and baptised that whining infant as reverently and solemnly as if he had been in a great
cathedral.

It must have been a strange scene in the " House
of the Murder"—the gaunt old man dripping from
the rain and the sea, holding the baby tenderly and
awkwardly, with the body of the mother lying beside
them. He gave the baby the name Patrick, the first

that came to him, "*Pathricius, ego te baptiso,*" and
so forth in his queer Latin brogue, and the small new
Christian howled dismally, and the gale answering
howled outside.

Then he unbuttoned the breast of his greatcoat
and fastened the baby inside—so that only its ridiculous red face could be seen—and started for home.
Crossing more easily this time, he found his old
horse huddled in dumb resignation under the lee of
the wall, and rode home through the storm at a good
pace with a light heart. Every now and then the
child cried to show that the life was in it, and then
he tried to quiet it tenderly with " Be hushed now,
vick machree, son of my heart! Ah! be sthill,
Pathrick. Be aisy, ye cantankerous little cur!"

There was great work that night in the little house,
when the old priest and his housekeeper welcomed
their guest. And when the baby was cosily asleep,
Peter got into his big armchair and mixed himself a
steaming tumbler of punch—for no man values
punch more, though of course in strict moderation—
and he felt he deserved it to-night. "An' would ye
believe it?" and at this point of his story his voice
shook with pathos—"would ye believe it, at th'
instant when I was putting it to me lips the clock
sthruck twelve, and so I couldn't taste a dhrop, not
a single dhrop!" For if he had tasted it after mid-

"PATHRICIUS, EGO TE BAPTISO"

night he could not have said Mass.   This was a lame
ending to his one adventurous night.

The baby was kept in the priest's house, and, when
the gale went down, the mother's body was brought
from the island and buried; I think Father Peter
found afterwards who she was, though her name
never passed his lips.

For nearly twelve years " Pathrick " has ruled the
priest's house, thriving under the rough tenderness
of Peter Flannery.   Meanwhile Peter has led always
the same life, rising in the early morning to say
Mass in the cold chapel before a scanty congregation
of women; many of them pray aloud with shut eyes
and entire disregard of their neighbours, and Patrick
now serves him as clerk, looking very serious in his
little white surplice like a Cupid in a monk's cowl.

Then he rides on his sick-calls, miles and miles
away through the bogs and over the hills, for he goes
at any hour of the day or night to any one who
chooses to summon him; or he walks down to the
school—where he usually finds Patrick standing in
the corner with his face to the wall, in disgrace—or
he goes his rounds through the Village of Moher.

Many a time have I seen him striding down the
Village "like an executioner," and the dirty little
ragged children running to meet him and snuggling

their smeared faces against his long coat. The first time babies see him they yell as if he was the Devil; but the next time they would yell louder still if he forgot to fondle them. Many a time have I seen him standing in the street, beleaguered by a cluster of women, scowling nervously over them and looking to see if there is any chance of rescue; while they all talk at once, quarrelling among themselves:

"Ah! Peggy Lonergan, dacint woman, be whisht, can't ye?"

"Mary Ronan, I take shame o' ye to be throublin' the holy priest so. Won't ye be lettin' me have a single word wid him?"

And now in the evenings he has something to dream about, and when he sits alone by the fire in his naked parlour, smoking his old pipe—with his tumbler of punch smoking too, to keep him company—he dreams of the great future of Patrick Flannery. He sees that urchin grow up a model, go to Maynooth and win prizes there, rise rapidly in the Church, and even become a Bishop. It is true Pat will have to change greatly before then, for it is a queer Bishop he would make now; but time works wonders and Pat has a good heart.

Peter hears him preaching the great sermons himself has never preached to the great congregations he has never seen. And he thinks that "His Lord-

ship Docthor Flannery" has a pleasing sound, that
Bishop Flannery will be
loved by all, that bles-
sings will go with him ;
it is he that will have
an eye for true worth
and never let a plain
man spend his life in
a wilderness while
smoother-tongued men
have all they want.

But at this point the
dream breaks, for he
knows in his heart that
he would be sorry to
leave his wilderness ; so
when the clock strikes
nine he slowly finishes

"WHEN WE WENT A-GIPSYING,
A LONG TIME AGO"

his punch, knocks out the ashes from his pipe, and
goes up the steep stairs to his bedroom, quavering in
his hoarse voice,

"When we went a-gipsying,
　A long time ago."

A CONNEMARA MIRACLE

"THE LAZIEST MAN IN CONNEMARA"

SOME said big John Murnane was the laziest man in Connemara, others called him a surly dog; but I always liked him. He had some excuse for his laziness and s u r l i n e s s. When I knew him first he was active enough. He used then to begin the day in the brightest of tempers, and if he had been let sit in peace and sunshine would have remained merry, but work undermined his cheerfulness. His farm lay high above Leenane at the head of the Killeries, a creek walled in by mountains, in the heart of the Irish Highlands.

Two roads wind down to the creek, one lower by Finigan's shebeen, and one by Murnane's farm. In those days I half envied him; he had a pretty little wife, a neat home, and three pigs, while I owned neither a pig nor a wife, he had no vain ambition and asked nothing better than to live and die at home in that wilderness.

But when I visited Connemara again, years later, things had changed with him; he had met with ill-luck, and had lost heart. A bank holding his little money had failed, his crops had failed too, his last pig had died; everything had gone badly with him. He spent half his time at the shebeen, and had a dangerous look. To make matters worse, he was to be turned out of his farm—had quarrelled with his landlord; for a true Galway-man always quarrels with the man best able to thrash him. Murnane was full of fight, his mother used to say of him that he was never at rest except when he was fighting, and of course he knew that some one else must be responsible for his misfortunes, so he laid the blame at his landlord's door.

His landlord was my friend Shane Desmond who in those days was always at war with his tenants. Here I thought were the makings of a tragedy—a lawless district, an unruly peasantry, and a hated landlord.

Well, that summer my stay in Connemara was brief, and soon after I left, Murnane came to the turning-point of his life. I have the story from his own lips.

In November, when the days grew short and the nights dark, there was a rumour in the shebeens near Leenane that some of " the boys " were coming from Desmond's estate in Clare, a fishing boat would bring them from Liscannor to the Killeries and take them back without any one being the wiser, and their trip might mend matters.

One boisterous evening, Murnane was standing at his window watching his wife trudging heavily up the mountain road. All day the wind had been hissing drearily through the mountains ; now it was snarling and yelping like fighting dogs. There was a veil of rain wavering on the grey crescent of sea.

He had spent hours that day at the shebeen. As he watched his wife he thought in a muddled way how pretty she was when she was young though now she was a plain little woman, he thought of the time when he first caught her in his arms, down yonder where the Owen-Erriff runs by the Devil's Mother Mountain—"I love ye, Molly Joyce! tell me now, are ye listenin' to me, mavourneen dheelish! I love ye!" —then of their life, of the careless years, of his losses and troubles, of the heavy evenings he spent smoking by the dull light of the turf-fire alone with her in this cabin, then of the loud nights in the shebeen, and of the dreary times at home after. She seemed to get so silent and dull, he was tired of her worried face, sick of her frightened way of watching him.

Though he knew that she was a kind little woman, and that she loved him like a dog, he had grown hard and cold with her. Only that evening he had told her roughly to stop making a hare of herself, moping and poking about doing nothing, and to get out of that and to spend the night at her father's; and she, knowing the little use of speaking to him, had gone silently. He felt half sorry for his roughness as he watched her; after all she was a good soul and they had been happy together once. But now that he was to lose his last belongings why should he keep her? how could he when he couldn't? She must go back to her own folk who were well-to-do— for those parts—while he went out to try his luck in the world.

Then he walked up and down his cabin. It looked wretched; the turf-fire on the hearth had smouldered, the whitewashed walls were blackened by smoke, they had little on them but a big crucifix, there was little furniture left. He remembered it bright and homelike; now it would be unroofed, he would be penniless and homeless unless Desmond was shot that night.

For the boat had come from Liscannor, and when Desmond drove back from Carrala, "the boys" were to wait for him on the lower road. If he came by the upper road, Murnane would see him, and was to put a light in his window; then they would change their ambush.

At the best, Murnane's thoughts were not clear. Now he kept thinking, over and over again, sure 'twas no harm lighting a candle, 'twas no business of his whatever the boys below might do; then, 'twas his chance of revenge, sure the man deserved to be killed; then, if only he was going to hit Desmond himself 'twould be different, but 'twas cowardly just lighting a candle; then, 'twas a black job after all.

Outside the twilight was fading; the wind was working itself into a rage with uncanny cries. Was that the wind or the shriek of the Banshee? It was said that lost souls were chained on the wind, surely

there were human cries in it now : why were the
dead abroad to-night ?

The landscape was blotted out. Then the moon
began to rise and the backs of the mountains rose
out of the darkness. Then he saw their steep
walls and the winding lane of slaty water between
them.

There was a glimmer of silver over Muilrea; the
moon floated into sight with milky-edged clouds
round her; a path of light crossed the water, and
three streams glittered on the Blue Gable Mountain.
The moon seemed to shine out with strange sudden-
ness; the jagged top of Muilrea stood black against
her, making her look as if a ragged piece had been
torn from her. He stared till the light dazzled him ;
then turned away.

The black crucifix on the wall opposite was shown
plainly by the moonlight ; the face of its figure was
bent forward as if watching him. He had prayed
before it so often all his life. It had seen him a
baby in the cradle, a child dandled by his mother, a
man bringing home his bride. Here in this cabin,
this one room where his life had been centred, the
crucifix hung as a silent witness. He thought of his
misery ; sure he had cause to hate the man. Still
that sad face was watching him, he could not bear it,
must take the crucifix down. Placing a bench under,

he reached to the nail fastening the top and wrenched it out.

The moon was covered. The cross leant forward in the darkness. He turned his head away to shun the bent face; and groping, tugged out the nail at the foot. The cross seemed as heavy as lead, he dared not look at it, placing it in the corner—face downward—he covered it with a cloth.

Then he stood again at the window. The moon shone out, and the wind lurched drunkenly against the door, with an echo of singing from the shebeen, the chorus of " Crúiscin Lan " (The Little Full Jug):

"Is gradh mo croidhe a cuilin ban ban ban,
 Is gradh mo croidhe a cuilin ban."

He could fancy the crowded smoky room, the glowing turf-fire, and old Pat Finigan singing with a jolly flushed face; and those other men listening too, crouching behind the low wall.

There was a stain of rust on his right hand and he thought it was blood, rubbed it but it was dry, felt as if a curse had fallen on him. Then came a pause between the gusts, and he heard the ring of hoofs on the stony road. At once he turned back to light the candle, took it with a shaky hand: then on the wall where the cross had been, saw a dazzling white cross.

He staggered back with his eyes fixed on it: it was a miracle, a last warning. He dashed the candle on the ground, and crunched it under foot into the earthen floor.

The moon was drowned by the clouds and left the cabin pitch dark. The wind crashed against the door again. He unlatched the door, it was dashed open—he could not breathe—tried to pull it to after him but could not, some unseen hand seemed dragging it. The wind swirled through the cabin and flung the cloth from the prostrate crucifix.

The next morning was calm, with a stainless sky. Molly came trudging down the mountain road from her father's farm, her heart heavy with foreboding. All that night she had been crying and praying. The glory of the morning, the rare colouring of the mountains, the green crescent of sea, were nothing to her.

As she reached the door of the cabin, she saw her man sitting by the hearth with his head bent forward on his hands. The crucifix was gone from its place. It had been fixed there when the walls had been shining with fresh whitewash, now they were blackened, but where it had hung the wall remained white in the shape of a cross.

"Is it you, asthore?" he said, came to meet her, put his hands on her shoulders, and drew her close to him.

"It's a hard world 'tis, mavourneen, but we'll bear God's will together, Molly dear."

SHANE DESMOND

CASTLE DESMOND faces seaward, so when the long
battlements show over the trees as you drive from
Liscannor to Lisdoonvarna you see only the back,
and they say in Moher Village, "the front of the
Castle is behind it." From the terrace in front you
can see the Cliffs of Moher and the wastes of the
Atlantic, and to the right the Arran Islands, with
the dim Connemara Mountains beyond them. The
Castle is a noble old house, with big panelled rooms,
wide stairs, and dark corridors; but when I stayed
there first—years ago—it was dreary, because Shane
Desmond was a pauper. He had a long rent-roll and
got no rents. He used to drive about the country
with loaded revolvers, and with a repeating rifle
strapped on his dog-cart. We christened him
"Shane" at school, when he was a patriot and was
eloquent on Ireland's wrongs and the heroism of
Shane O'Neill. But he ceased to be a patriot when
he became a landlord.

While Cornelius Desmond lived, Moher was merry; few paid him rent, but that mattered little, as he never paid a debt. When "Ould Corney" died, Moher was managed by an agent who was known as "The Snipe" because no one could ever succeed in shooting him. So when Shane came of age he inherited Corney's debts and the hatred earned by "The Snipe."

As Shane is my friend I have a keen eye for his faults; chief of them is a perilous temper though you could find no man more cheery and kindly. But it is absurd to see how easily some manage him; his sister Aileen can turn him round her little finger. I was in love with Aileen Desmond in those days— or thought I was—so in my eyes she was perfect. Some people saw nothing wonderful in her; but I would have been sorry for them if they had owned that in Moher. The folk there loved her as much as they hated Shane; you would have known it seeing how they brightened when they met her, with "a kind good mornin' to ye, Miss Aileen," or how they watched her in the chapel on Sundays as if they were saying their prayers to her, and small blame to them! for in those days she was a saint, an angel, and a goddess, and had many other incompatible charms, and the stones she trod on and the trees by the wayside worshipped her as she went by.

I remember she had a depraved terrier named Mike. I hated to see her fondle him though of course I pretended to love him.

Shane was fond of Aileen in a patronising brotherly way, but was devoted to a small white American, Virginia K. Geraldine, commonly called Kitty. Kitty Geraldine was staying with the Blakes of Ballynahinch, over beyond Ennistimon, and all the young men of County Clare were at her feet. Ballynahinch swarmed with loud "Squireens" and ferocious Police Inspectors and swaggering boys from the barracks at Ennis. I am not saying that they were only after her money, for indeed she was very taking; nor am I calling her a flirt, though she fooled half the manhood of Clare. I dare not risk vexing her, for—as they say in Moher—when Shane is in a rage lions are lambs to him. He spent half his time dangling after her and scowling at her other admirers; and when he came home his moods were something to remember. I wonder when I think how much I stood from him in those days; but then I was in love with his sister.

Well, one day Kitty treated him worse than usual; so after spending an hour or so frowning at every one else, he said "Good-bye," sternly and gruffly, to Mrs. Blake—a kind old soul who was always like a mother to him—and strode off without even a look for Kitty.

She seemed to mind little, and there was a glimmer
of a twinkle in her quiet grey eyes. He drove his
dog-cart home at a breakneck pace, making the
pebbles fly, and his road lay through Moher Village.

The Village, a narrow street of thatched cabins,
lies hard by the Cliffs of Moher, on the road that
runs northward from Liscannor to Lisdoonvarna.
The pigs and poultry there spend most of their time
blocking the street, and in those days there was one
old fellow—Dan McCaura by name—who seemed to
live in it.

When Shane came clattering through the Village,
the pigs and the poultry fled; but Dan was too late
and was knocked down. He was more frightened
than hurt, but I have been told that from the noise
he made as he was being carried into his cabin you
would have thought he had been killed. All the
people of Moher were in a state of delightful excitement; so were the poultry, only the pigs were
indifferent. Shane came home that night raging
against everybody and chiefly against old Dan.

Now the Moher folk were so excited at first that
they felt quite friendly to Shane Desmond; but when
they calmed down they took another view of him.
They felt he was going too far; did he think they
were the dust under his feet? Wasn't it enough

that he should evict them and trample on them? Wouldn't he even leave them their lives? There were bitter words that night in the group round the fire in the shebeen; all Shane's misdeeds were raked up with threats and curses.—"The curse of the crows on him!" "May the daisies be his quilt!" "May the grass grow before his door!" "Didn't the boys wait for him one night at Leenane, an' 'twas he only escaped them by goin' home the wrong road, the Divil sweep him!"

Most of the men were too loud to be dangerous— the loudest was Larry Ronan the blacksmith, a man who never hurt a fly—but there was one black-looking fellow, young Michael McCaura, the victim's grandson, who sat on a barrel in the shadow watching the angry faces red in the glow of the turf-fire, and felt that it was for him to see to this, and took the threats as reproaches. All he said was—"An' mebbe he won't have the same luck next time."

Mike McCaura, like the rest of the Moher folk, worshipped Aileen. She was very kind to him, she liked all her "own people," all the old familiar faces in her wild home. But when Mike saw that kind smile of hers—it would have melted a stone—and heard her "Good morning, Michael"—she had a wheedling brogue that would have moved mountains (Irish mountains, anyway)—then he went on brighter and better. In his heart he believed that she had a weakness for him, and as long as he could remember —ever since the time when she was a child, and he a bare-footed ragamuffin proud to hold her pony for her—she had been a queen to him.

In the chapel he never took his eyes off her; Father Flannery's eloquence was lost on him, for he spent his time day-dreaming how when he found the treasure the monks buried in the bog at Liscannor, or the three tall galleons of the Armada that lie lost in the sea off Spanish Point, or the diamond mine— undiscovered mines of diamonds and gold are plentiful in the Irish hills—he would marry " Miss Aileen." He must have had great belief in the power of wealth, for his looks were against him; he had a dark and hard face, and though not tall was heavily built with great shoulders and big square hands. He was a man of few words, though it was said he was eloquent at times. If Shane were dead, Aileen would rule over Moher, and there would be fair days for every one.

McCaura made up his mind to shoot Desmond, and was proud of the resolve. He was a hero in his own eyes when he started next evening with a gun and a bottle of whisky hidden under his long coat, and was in high spirits though it was misty and cheerless weather. He took up his post in the

shrubbery on the left side of the avenue, close to the
big gate of the Castle. The shrubbery was a tangle;
in those days the dust and injury of age lay heavy
on the Castle, and grass grew on the drive. Shane
was at Ennistimon Fair, and when he came back
would stop just inside the gate, while Doherty, his
old coachman, got down and locked it. The gate
lodge was then empty, and there were only four
servants in the Castle.

Mike crouched among the bushes, with the gun by
him, and plied himself with whisky. Through the
branches he could see dimly the white top of the gate,
and on it the crest, a "lion rampant," an absurd beast
standing on one leg; it was supposed to be defiant,
but now its lifted paws seemed giving an excited
warning. The whisky at first softened Mike, and
as he looked at the lion he felt it was a pity to kill
one of the old stock, the real gentry, now that half
Ireland was owned by upstarts and money-lenders.
There was never a Desmond shot before except in
battles or duels—they were grand folk in the old
times—but 'twas the man's own fault, why couldn't
he live and let live? Sure they wanted nothing
better than to be friends with him, if only he would let
them alone. But a further drink steeled his heart,
also his temper grew savage, for his hiding-place was
unpleasant, his knees sank into the mud, at every

move the stiff wet laurel leaves and branches worried him. He began to have doubts whether Desmond was coming and was angry with him for being late.

By the time it grew dark, Mike was muddled and desperate. Then suddenly he heard light steps on the gravel, some one was coming down the avenue, then a terrier rushed into the shrubbery, barking.

His first thought was to strangle the dog, but it kept out of his reach; he was mortally afraid it would knock against the trigger of the gun.

The steps on the gravel stopped, and then his heart stopped too, for he heard Aileen's wheedling voice:

"Are you in there, Mike? Come out of that now this minute!"

He did not know whether he was standing on his heels or his head. How did she know he was there? It was all up with him! But then she had never called him "Mike" before, she had never spoken to him so lovingly. He could not believe his ears, then heard Aileen again:

"Mike, dear, don't you hear me calling you? Are you there, Mike?"

He got up and lurched heavily into the avenue before her.

"I am so, Miss," he said.

There was once a man who rubbed an old ring, and was surprised to find that he had raised the Devil. So was Aileen astonished when she called her terrier out of the shrubbery, and found she had raised a hulking peasant. Then, when she saw it was only Michael McCaura, she laughed with great enjoyment. Now, it was worth walking a mile to hear Aileen's laugh, but just then Mike had a dazed fear that she was laughing at him, for, when he stood before her, he realised that he was drunk, could not speak, his legs were walking from under him, the earth and the trees were tottering, only Aileen's trim figure was steady.

Aileen was telling him that she had been calling her terrier, that she had come down to meet her brother, and how sorry she was that Dan had been hurt; but her words were meaningless to him. He only knew that she was calling him " Michael " now, and speaking in her accustomed sweet high and mighty way, though a minute before she had called him " Mike," as if she cared for him. But how could she care for him when he was blind drunk? He wished that the earth would open and swallow him. Next day he had only a vague idea how he got home, only remembered that, as he shambled away, the terrier sent a hurricane of derisive barks after him; but he found the gun still in the

c

shrubbery; and later he came to be glad that she
stopped him.

McCaura told me part of this story when I came
on him strangely afterwards, a long way from
Liscannor. But I knew nothing of it in the old
days, when I was in love with Aileen Desmond.

"THE OTHER COUNTRY"

I HAD this story from an old peasant, on a hill by
Renvyle in Connemara. He knew the folk-lore of
Connemara by heart—all manner of grim and uncanny
legends—and began each story with "I do be
hearin'" or "They do be sayin'," but this he said
was true, he had been a witness himself.

"Ghosts?" said he, "that's all foolishness and ould
women's tales. But the folk come back, the folk themselves; that's thrue, so it is. There was Bridget Joyce
that lived by Maamtrasna, 'twas a week she'd been
buried, and her babe was pinin' an' cryin' for her all
the nights long. Her man he wakes up one night
wontherin' why the babe was sthill, an' there sat
Bridget herself, an' she cuddlin' it in her arms. Her
man he daren't say a word to her, afeard she'd be
goin'; he lies there not takin' his eyes off her. An'
when the day broke she put the child by, an' went
out wid niver a look for him that had been mighty

fond of her. An' ould Michael Mulcahy, that was a
herd up yonther, on the Blue Gable Mountain—a lone
ould man he was, an' cared for nobody in the world
but the sheep he herded—he'd been long dead when
drunken John Meehan, that was herd afther him and
took small heed o' the sheep, he goes on the Mountain
one night, an' he sees ould Michael herdin' them,
afeard they'd be fallin', the craythurs. Is it where
the folk come back from? sure from th' Other
Counthry? Is it where's th' Other Counthry? ah,
but that's more than than the likes o' me knows.
Mebbe 'tis the Vanishin' Island that the folk do be
seein'. Annyway, 'tis where they live when they're
dead. More by token, when I was a gossoon I saw
one that came back. 'Twas Phaudrig Coyne—a
mild aisy man he was, for all he was big—he did
use to live in that farm down yonther, 'twixt
Ardnagreeva an' Cashleen." (Here he pointed to a
brown cabin close to the sea; it looked like a haystack
in the distance.)

"Phaudrig Coyne he'd been dead a year an' more;
an' young Mrs. Coyne—a purty an' bright woman
she was—she marries drunken John Meehan, the
herd, and takes him to live in the farm yonther.
'Twas the gran' weddin' an' dancin' like mad afther
it, wid lashins o' dhrink; there was scarce room to
sthand in the farm, all the counthry had come

though 'twas a wild rainin' night. Meself an' th'
other chilther an' th' ould folk were huddled agin
the wall, and ivery one else dancin' while there was
breath in them. The table 'twas pushed aside by
the hearth ; two fiddlers an' a blind piper was on chairs
on the table, all playin' like for dear life. The room
was full o' dust kicked up from th' earth o' the floor.
'Twas wontherful the noise o' the clogs an' the playin',
whiles the house seemed to shake wid it and wid the
storm outside till ye'd have thought the bacon
flitches 'd have been fallin' from the rafters. 'Twas
terrible warm too, for there was a big turf-fire on the
hearth. I'd niver seen as manny candles afore—all
of a row they were on the chimney—an' the folk
jigged an' jumped in rows facin' one another, an' them
that looked towards the candles had their faces lit,
an' th' others had their faces dark ; 'twas mighty fine
watchin' them an' the quare shadows jiggin' an
jumpin' on the walls. Sudden comes a loud knock
at the door. 'Come in,' cried young Mrs. Coyne—
Mrs. Meehan I mane—breathless she was, 'come in,
then, whoiver y'are, all Ireland 'd be welcome to-
night.' She goes on jiggin' agin. A big man
comes in wid 'God save all here!' The candles was
nigh blow out by the wind, the rain splashed in on
us, an' the room filled wid shmoke from the turf-fire
when the door opened. The man looks round—for

the life o' me I couldn't think who he was, I knew
I'd seen him afore—nobody else heeds him. He
slips quiet 'twixt two rows of dancers, an' he sits
down on the bench that was afore the fire by the
table. He sthoops forrard houldin' his hands over
the turf; he looked mighty cold an' tired, there was
thick mud on his boots, his frieze coat was soppin'
an' his hair was caked by the rain. He poked the
fire wid his foot; it blazed up, throwin' red light on
his face an' his hands. Young Mrs. Coyne—Meehan
I mane—went on jiggin' just behind him, wid her
hands on her hips.

"Ould Mrs. Coyne—a little shiverin' woman she
was, wid a squealin' voice—she gets up from where
she was squattin' in a corner, she goes hobblin' an'
tottherin' along by the wall lanin' on her sthick—
there was scarce room for her to pass—till she
sthands by the man; she put out her left hand,
shakin' twas like a leaf, an' she lays it on his head.
Says she, 'Ye're welcome home agin, Phaudrig
Coyne, me son. 'Tis the sore time you've been from
us.' The man he never moves, he sthoops there,
an' a power o' stheam comin' from his drenched
sthockins. Young Mrs. Meehan she bursts out
laughin' and sthops dancin', she goes an' sthands
near the man on his left side. 'You'll be excusin'
her, sir,' says she, 'she's terrible ould, she's afther

"WASN'T IT ON THIS TABLE YE WERE WAKED?"

thinkin' you're her son.' The man he starts at her voice; he leans back from the fire wid his left elbow on the table. 'Her son?' says he. He looks round and up at young Mrs. Meehan. (Then I could see his face full; terrible sad he looked, an' there was no spark in his eyes; his eyes were dead, ay, though they were wide open an' seein' ye they were dead.) 'Her son?' says he, 'an' why not? I am so,' says he. Mrs. Meehan, that hadn't seen his face till then, she turns whiter than milk, she screeches, all the folk sthop dancin', the fiddlers sthop playin', only the bagpipes went on, for the piper, bad luck to him! was blind, and he was blowin' that hard that he wouldn't have heard the Last Thrumpet. Mrs. Meehan she clutches hould o' the table like she was fallin'. 'What's this mane?' she says chokin'. 'Is it afther a joke y'are? or is that you, Phaudrig? Can it be you, Phaudrig? Wasn't it on this table ye were waked? Ah, man alive, don't ye know that ye're dead?' 'Dead or alive,' squeals th' ould mother, putthin' her arm round his neck and lanin' on him—she was no taller than him though he was sittin'—'dead or alive, ye're welcome home, Phaudeen acushla.'

"Phaudrig he looks roun' over his left shoulther at the folk—they were huddled at the far end o' the room, they didn't look half so manny as when they

were dancin'—all stharin' at him, manny were the
white faces turned to him; some o' the women were
prayin' aloud, the fiddlers on the table were that
frightened they daren't get down, but th' ould fool of
a blind piper goes on playin' a reel just the same,
burstin' his cheeks. Phaudrig he looks roun', an' ye
could hear the folk on the left side o' the room gaspin'
when they met his eyes. He looks back at his
wife—'Dead?' says he, 'I am so—worse luck!'
'Phaudeen,' says th' ould mother that was houldin'
him that tight you'd have thought he was gold, 'tell
me, Phaudeen alanna, is it in Hell or in Heaven
y'are?' 'An' where would I be,' says Phaudrig,
'but where all the folk are—in th' Other Counthry?
There they are, th' ould folk that have been dead
ages ago. 'Tis the same life over agin—ah! God
pity us all!—aich lives as he lived here over agin,
wid little to ate an' little aise. 'Tis a counthry like
this same, rocky an' hard an' there's no kindness in
the hills, an' we go a-fishin' on black and wild nights.'
John Meehan, who was dhrunk, he sthaggers across
the room (his eyes were near shut like as if he was
asleep, an' he spoke as if he'd an egg in his mouth).
He slaps Phaudrig on the back. 'Cheer up, Phaudrig,
me man,' says he, 'for why are ye so glum? Sure a
heavy heart seldom combs a grey head. No man
shall be glum on me weddin' night, an' I marryin'

your wife.' Phaudrig he looks up at his wife. 'Is that so?' says he very quiet; he was always a mild man. She says nothin'; she looks near as dead as himself. All the time the bagpipes go on playin' the reel. Phaudrig goes on, 'I'll be askin' your pardon, ma'am. I'd not have come if I'd known,' says he. He sthands up an' looks round at the folk—ye could hear them gaspin' agin when they met his eyes. 'Ye needn't be so afeard, good people,' says he, very quiet like, 'ye were glad enough to be friends with me once.' He sthoops down an' kisses his little ould mother, he goes an' opens the door, there was a terrible great noise o' the wind an' the say, the wind rushes in wid rain drenchin' the most of us, the room filled wid shmoke from the fire, all the candles were blown out. His ould mother she hobbles tot-therin' afther him, squealin', 'Ah! for God's sake take me wid ye, acushla. Don't be leavin' me behind ye, Phaudeen.' But he goes out from the door "

BY THE DEVIL'S MOTHER

WHEN I was in Connemara last summer, I drove from
Westport to Leenane, and had to start early in the
morning. There was an Irish-American at the hotel
—a big over-dressed fellow—who was going the
same way, so we shared a car; we sat on one side of
it and our luggage was piled on the other. When I
first set eyes on him he was swaggering in front of
the hotel, whistling "Come back to Erin," and I
took a dislike to him at once. I would rather have
had the car to myself, and he seemed aggressively
friendly. I was too sleepy to talk and was ill-
tempered for the morning was keen and misty; it
was dreary work driving through invisible scenery,
Clew Bay was hidden and we could only see the foot
of Croagh-Patrick. But the man was irrepressible,
no coldness of mine could chill him, he was more
garrulous than rooks. He tried vainly to get into
talk with the driver—a withered peevish little man,
with scanty black whiskers—then he turned back to

me, for because I was nearer I fell an easier victim. He seemed in great spirits and that angered me the more, and he talked only of himself. His speech was elaborately American, he revelled in strange phrases as if he was crying to the world that he was no slave of England but a citizen of the Great Republic—I never heard an American speak so except in English comedies—yet the twang had a quaint echo of the old ineradicable brogue.

I hardly listened to him but could not help learning that his name was Corrigan, that he was of Connemara by birth—he seemed to think this would astound me—and that his folk lived in a valley by Aasleagh, "The Jagged Valley." He told me how he had gone out penniless, had found strong friends and strange luck in New York, and now after seven years' exile was well-to-do with a sure hope of riches. He had prospered by means of a " corner store "; I did not trouble to ask what that was, for I am so hopelessly poor that I care little how others make money. And just then we drove past a boggy field where there was a multitude of tiny round spider-webs linking the tips of the long grass and shimmering because the dew was thick on them, roofing the field with delicate silk. So I lost much of Corrigan's history.

But soon after that—as we were driving through

a wide bog towards a barrier of mountains—the day brightened, the mists rose and my spirits with them, and I began to take a new interest in life and in Corrigan. And after all—I said to myself—after all, if I was as young and with as good cause to be happy as this boy who went out sorrowful and is now coming again with rejoicing, instead of being an old fogey with small reason to be hopeful or proud, who knows but I might be as confiding? As the day grew clearer I began to find him more likable; he seemed a fellow of a bright nature, only too trusting and warm-hearted. Clouds were still about, but the morning gave promise of the weather I like best in Connemara, weather when on one hand the mountains are brown under a scowl of clouds and on the other hand they have splendid colours and there is sunshine and a blue sea.

Corrigan was holding forth on the sameness of Connemara, as if he thought that because he had changed the mountains should have changed also. It was on just such a morning, he said, that he jogged northwards along this same road in his father's jolting cart, with his worldly goods tied in a bundle. Now he was returning so altered, seeing everything with such different eyes, and yet nothing was changed; the children staring open-mouthed from the doors of the thatched cabins or running

after our car begging and catching the coins he
threw to them—I think he had filled his pockets
with pence—the dogs barking as we passed, the
little pigs scurrying with shrieks from under the
horse's hoofs, he could have sworn they were all the
same. He only hoped (and here he spoke with some
feeling and partly forgot his American accent) he
only hoped that he would find as little change in his
home in the Jagged Valley, and in a girl who used
to live yonder by the Devil's Mother Mountain.

At this I pricked up my ears, for because I am an
old bachelor I like sentiment: I mean I like it in
others. There was a girl—he went on, speaking
half jocularly but I could see the matter lay very
near to his heart—there was a girl—Maureen
Cavanagh by name—who lived in The Old Hag's
Glen under the shadow of the Devil's Mother Mountain; her cheeks were like bramble roses, and her
eyes were as blue as the sea in fine weather. Corrigan and she were lovers, and since they were both as
poor as the dead, were eager to marry. But the old folk
forbade it, for the Connemara peasants are mercenary,
and marriage there is almost as much a matter of
bargain as in cities. So instead of waiting to in-
herit his father's cabin and pig, he went to America
in search of a fortune. He parted from Maureen
with the usual vows of constancy, though in his eyes

they were needless for he was so sure of his own
truth that he was sure also of her.   Besides, she had
already been faithful to him for over three months
and had loyally snubbed a rich neighbour who spent
half his time making sheep's eyes at her.   Of course
they both knew that he was sure to come back in a
year or so with his pockets bursting with dollars, so
Maureen said that she would wait for him for ever if
need be, and that if he grew old before he grew rich, .
and came back grey-haired and deaf, he would find
her grey-haired—and perhaps deaf—but still waiting.
He was not to write to her, he was but a slow hand
at a pen, and she a still poorer scholar, and the
letters would anger her father.

During each year of his exile he had hoped that
the next Spring would see him homeward bound.
He had written at times to the old folk, but not
often, for what was there to write about?   He heard
from them sometimes when they got a neighbour to
write for them or sent messages through friends.
They never mentioned Maureen, but sure " no news
was good news."   All these years he had been
constant—he seemed to pride himself on this as if
any girl of his acquaintance would have jumped at
the chance of marrying him—and now he would
take Maureen away. it was a noble welcome she
would meet in New York. she would be a fine lady

with silk dresses and diamonds and luxuries beyond all her dreams.

He could not believe, he said, that to-day he would see her and the old folk. First he was going home to the Jagged Valley, his old mother he knew would be sitting cowering over the turf-fire trying to keep warm—she was so sickly that she did little else all day except heap shrill querulous abuse on her husband, whom she worshipped—and the old man would be patiently and feebly digging in his acre by the cabin, tilling the rocks. Glad and proud the old folk would be, seeing him; his mother would be half afraid to hug him, and he such a fine gentleman; his father would talk to him with a power of respect. A good time would begin for them now, after their long lives of work and want they could sit easy. He would see that they were well cared for after he left them; he knew that not all the gold of Vanderbilt could tempt them away from the Jagged Valley.

Then after dining, he said, after dining on potatoes and bacon at his father's rickety table, he would walk round to the Old Hag's Glen, taking the bridle-path behind the Devil's Mother, it was a rough path and crossed half a dozen streams on stepping-stones but it would bring him to the back of Cavanagh's farm so he could surprise Maureen. She would be spinning, sitting at the door of the smoky cabin to

D

have light for her work, and looking up every now
and then towards the path through the rocks. He
would look through the little side-window at the
gable-end of the cabin—the window was so dirty you
could not have seen through it, only luckily a pane
had been broken a long time ago—many times he
had laughed to see her spinning, with the light from
the door on her, and looking wistful because he was
long coming.

By this time he had wholly forgotten his American
accent and had the right brogue. We had left the
bog and were driving close under the wall of mountains, nearing the Devil's Mother. Suddenly he
gripped my arm: " An' there it is," he said, " there's
th' Ould Hag's Glen, you'll not be seein' the Farm
for 'tis round the corner o' the Mountain." We were
passing the mouth of a rocky gap so squeezed by
mountains that it was a well of shadows and looked
as if no sunlight could reach it.

Corrigan stared up the Glen breathlessly. In a
minute we were past it and driving under the Devil's
Mother. The side of the Mountain was a miracle of
colouring, lit by patches of purple and gold where
heather and furze blossomed, and fringed by tassels
of wild fuchsia.

Just where the road curves between the Devil's
Mother and the Blue Gable Mountain, a little girl—

about five years old, I thought—jumped from a heap of stones where she had been seated waiting for passing cars. I have never seen a prettier child; she had blue eyes of a singular colour, like an old porcelain, and a tangle of shadowy brown hair. Her bare legs were red with cold and one of her feet had been cut by a stone.

She ran after us calling out, " Ah, give me a penny, kind gintlemen ! me mother is dyin' at home an' me six little brothers an' sisthers are stharvin'." She had a voice like a bell and the most lovable of brogues.

Corrigan started when he saw her ; I noticed how he stared back at her. He flung her a big silver coin—a dollar I think—she stooped to pick it up, and then was hidden by a spur of the Mountain.

" 'Tis a quare thing," he said to me, " 'tis a quare thing, but I've gone half the world over wid blue eyes, the moral of that child's, in me heart an' niver meetin' the like o' them. An' here at home the very children that beg by the roadside have Maureen's eyes. Now whose child might that be ? " he said to the driver.

" She's Dan Doherty's only child, that lives behind the Glen yonther."

" What ! Misther Doherty is it ? Bad luck to him ! " said Corrigan.

"Every day of her life, rain or shine," the driver went on, "she's here beggin', an' her mother she begs by the brow o' yonther hill. An' why not? would ye be havin' them stharve? Ye wouldn't think it, but Mrs. Doherty she was the finest girl in Connemara, so she was; an' she married Dan because he was rich, 'twas a great farm he had. Now he's lost iverythin', and he's dhrunk half the day long, dhrunk on their earnin's; 'tis luck for him that he has the two o' them to keep him, so it is."

"Is it Misther Doherty?" said Corrigan. "Ah! the poor fellow!"

Here there was a steep hill, so we got down from the car. As we walked up—"There," said the driver, "there Mrs. Doherty is," pointing to a woman, sitting huddled under a big bush of flowering wild fuchsia. Seeing us she stood up; I could not believe she was young. She was bent like an old woman, and wasted with misery; her face was half hidden by her shawl, her clothes were rags, her bare feet were black with mud. Without raising her eyes she stretched out her thin dirty hand to Corrigan who was nearest.

"For the merciful God's sake," she said, "give me a penny, fine gentleman! Me man he is dyin', me six little chilther are stharvin'!"

Corrigan stopped short. "Oh! My God!" he said with a sob in his voice,

"GIVE ME A PENNY, FINE GENTLEMAN!"

He had grown limp and white; all the swagger and jolliness had gone out of him. The beggar-woman looked up at him; then she shrank back as if she was terrified. He grasped her hand.

"God help ye, woman," he said, "an' is that you Maureen Cavanagh?"

The driver touched my shoulder. "Jump up on the car, sir," he said, "an' we'll be goin' on a bit." I got up and we drove on at a fair pace, neither of us looking back. I tried to set the driver talking of the couple we had left behind, but he was testy and silent, and seemed to think that I, a stranger, had no right to pry into their misfortune. He left Corrigan's luggage at Aasleagh, about a mile from the Devil's Mother.

Travelling back a month later from Leenane to Westport, on a wet morning, I had a more chatty driver. He told me much about Corrigan, speaking of him as "a dacint kind lad." Corrigan, I found, had gone on later to the old folk in the Jagged Valley; they had hardly known him, he was so well dressed and so dull; he had left them money and had then driven straight back to Westport. "And I do be hearin'," the driver said, "that Corrigan he offered Maureen Doherty all the money he had in the world—barrin' what th' ould folk needed—sayin'

that he was going sthraight home to New York, an'
she could buy back Doherty's farm, an' she an' the
child sthop beggin'. But Maureen she said that
she'd stharve a hunthred times afore takin' a penny
from him."

Just then we were passing the Devil's Mother,
and a child ran out from under a tree. She had a
dripping shawl over her, the rain had so wetted her
face that she looked as if she was crying, her bare
feet pattered on the road and splashed in the puddles.
It was the child with the wonderful blue eyes. She
ran after us, calling out, "Ah, give me a penny, kind
gentleman!"

COLONEL HERCULES DESMOND

COLONEL Hercules Desmond is the only man in the wide world who hates the Reverend Peter Flannery. Peter could not hate Judas, but he dislikes Hercules Desmond.

"Sir," said the Colonel to me, "that Father Flannery is a boor, a mischief-maker, a firebrand, and a disgrace to the Church."

"The Colonel," said Father Peter, another time, "the Colonel is a hard man, a cruel landlord. God forgive me for sayin' it! but he's a disgrace to the name of Desmond."

The Colonel prides himself on being of the old school; he can remember the end of the good days when Irishmen were not ashamed of fighting or drinking, those remote times before the Great Famine. If you meet him at Castle Desmond and set him talking over the wine and walnuts, in the big dining-room, he will tell you of the old doings

till you forget you are in our vexed Ireland and the
room fills with the ghosts of our forefathers—who
were strong in their time, and had warm blood in
them—crowding to hear some talk of their memory
in these cold days when they are mainly despised or
forgotten. Then the Desmonds portrayed along the
walls of the dining-room come to life and seem
trying to slip out of their dingy frames and take
their places at the long table where once they used
to sit singing and drinking till they lay quietly drunk
under it and the servants carried them to bed—in
the good times.

When it is winter and the logs blaze on the wide
hearth, the firelight catches one portrait of a big
red man in rich purple and lace, Sir Hercules Desmond—"fighting Hercules," a noted duellist and a
wild liver once—God rest his soul! for when he was
alive he never knew what rest meant. Then you find
it easy to believe that Sir Hercules, the fighter, has
come to life in the old Colonel, who would look right
well in that same purple and lace with a full-blown
periwig, and with a three-cornered hat set jauntily on
the side of his head. Indeed, he is out of place in
these precise days when gentlemen are afraid to
swagger, though he would have been the pride of
his country if he had flourished a hundred and fifty
years ago.

He is slow to talk of himself or of his soldiering—
when he fought before Sebastopol, not without glory
—but grows easily eloquent on the duels of Major
Theophilus Blake or of Lord Theobald Butler, and
the old-world traditions of Castle Desmond, and
those later revels when his brother Corney—dead
years ago now—was young and riotous. Sometimes
I try to fancy him as a spruce officer, but it is hard,
for he wears the dingiest of clothes, chiefly he loves
a faded shooting jacket and weather-beaten gaiters,
he is loyal to old clothes and old customs.

There is only one deed of his life that he is sorry
to remember—I am not saying his life has been
either prudish or proper—and it is on account of
this one misdeed that he hates Peter Flannery.

The Colonel lives in a small, square, white house,
out on the desolate cliffs between Lahinch and Liscannor. He is the landlord of a number of wretched
cabins scattered here and there on the road through
Liscannor bog, a kind landlord to tenants who
grovel before him, but stern if he meets undue inde-
pendence. He holds that a landlord should be a
king to his tenantry; he is all the prouder because
he is so poor, and expects "his inferiors" to cringe
bareheaded, as in the time when he says "it was
worth while to be born a gentleman."

I remember he had a great battle with his tenants over the seaweed. It was a bitter winter and they had the audacity to come, without asking his leave, and gather the seaweed floating round the rocks near his house. They refused to pay him anything for it, saying that the weeds growing in the Atlantic belonged to no one. Yet his housekeeper told me that while he was raging and threatening to evict every man on the estate, he was pinching himself and stinting his few luxuries—for money is very scarce in the square white house—to buy food for his tenants.

But the great struggle of his late days has been the Battle of the Well. The Well stands by the wayside just inside the Colonel's Park; all the neighbours drew water from it. Some said a Fairy lived in it; others said it was a Holy Well blessed by some forgotten saint, when Ireland was holy, though of course it was not to be compared with St. Bridget's Well over beyond Liscannor. Why, every one knows that, quite lately—a hundred years or so ago—St. Bridget's Well turned into blood and moved of its own accord to the other side of the road, because a woman dared to wash clothes in it.

Now the Colonel's Park was only a scanty plantation of scraggy saplings; they were sacred in his eyes, he had planted them himself, dreaming that they would yet rival the great trees over at Castle Desmond, but the sea-wind was too much for them. He had made up his mind that only for the neighbours those trees would be giants, but how

"MEN HAD BEEN SHOT FOR LESS"

could they thrive when half the bog-trotters in Clare came tramping through the Park on their way to the Well? So he decided to save his trees by closing the Well; he built a fence round it, and barred the way with a locked gate.

This tyrannous outrage set Clare on fire. A deputa-
tation of the more prominent citizens of the bog
marched on the square white house, but the despot
refused to see them. He said he was tired of
deputations. Every shebeen from Kinvarra to Kilkee
rang with eloquence. Yet no one knew what should
be done. Larry Ronan, the blacksmith of Moher,
said that men had been shot for less; but no one
heeded him. It was felt that this was scarcely a
shooting matter, and I think every one had at heart
a kind feeling for " ould Herc'les." If it had been
his nephew, Shane, it would have been another
thing.

There was no use trying to frighten the Colonel;
it would be easier to frighten the Devil—sure *He*
was afraid of holy-water. When " the boys " wanted
to frighten Crowe of Crowe Castle, they marched in
a solemn deputation, and hung three ill-fated crows
before his hall-door; but the Colonel would not
mind if you hung all the birds in County Clare, and
if you dug a grave before his hall-door the odds were
that he would put you into it.

So it was decided to appeal to the Parish-priest,
the Reverend Peter Flannery. Now Father Peter
hates politics and wrangling of all kinds; though
sometimes his heart smites him, for he feels that he
owes it to his great position as the parish-priest of

Moher to be at the head of everything, and not only
the father but the ruler of his people. But how can
that be if he keeps aloof from their struggles? And
he has a grudge against Hercules Desmond, who—
though he calls himself a Catholic—yet lives like a
heathen Turk.

Once, when Father Flannery preached a sermon
against him, Hercules swaggered out of the chapel,
to the deep scandal (and secret delight) of the whole
congregation, and chiefly of those who were kneeling
in the churchyard because there was no room indoors.
The old priest—erect on the altar-steps in full
vestments—grew scarlet at such sacrilegious dis-
respect; he broke down in his sermon, and had more
than half a mind to excommunicate Hercules on the
spot.

Father Peter—with all his gentleness—felt that
such an insult to him, a dignitary of The Church, in
his own chapel, in the face of his own people, was a
thing hard to forget; why, it was an insult to The
Church. As a man—a Ballyvaughan man—he has
deep respect for the Desmonds; as a priest he looks
—in vain—to them to bow down before him.

So when the deputation appealed to him, he could
not help welcoming it with a heart and a half. It
was wonderful what a public-spirited indignation
he felt against the Colonel's tyranny; though he

would have been ashamed to give way to a private
grudge.   He decided at once to place himself at the
head of his people, and fight the battle of the poor
against the cruelty of the rich.   The fact was that
the Colonel was in the wrong and had no legal right
to close the Well; though the tenants were partly in
the wrong, too, for they had certainly damaged his
dying trees.

Next day, a monster deputation marched on the
square white house; I met it coming along the road
through Liscannor bog, just at the spot where
Dark Andy, the blind beggarman, is said to have long
talks with the Headless Man, an affable familiar
ghost.

On either side of the road lay a long stretch
of peat-bog, and in the background wavered the
lines of low heathery hills, the nearer were green,
the further were brown.   It was a bright windy day.
and nimble shadows of clouds were drifting over the
hills and the bogs.

Father Flannery walked silently at the head of
the procession ; he could not have looked sterner or
graver if he had been face to face with death.   A
little behind him came two old bent men, dressed in
the fashion of knee-breeches and swallow-tailed
coats that will soon survive only in the English
" comic " press.   Next marched the Colonel's tenants

from their cabins by the quaking bog or on the
bare hill-side.   Larry Ronan, the blacksmith—one of

"DARK ANDY AND THE HEADLESS MAN"

Shane's tenants—was leading them, talking loudly
and brandishing a great hammer.   Behind came a
throng of neighbours, who had nothing to do with
the dispute, and little Patrick Flannery, who ought

E

to have known better, brought up the rear playing on a tin-kettle.

When they reached the new locked gate they halted, and Father Flannery made them a speech, bare-headed. I was too far off to hear what he said, but I know I caught the words Freedom and Tyranny, he was terribly in earnest. The brisk wind blew his white hair back; the old man looked noble standing out against the green background with his people, his " children," round him; he looked like a covenanting minister preaching before a battle.

When he stopped there was a dead silence. He turned to Ronan and took the big hammer from him, swung it up slowly with both hands—really he did it with a wonderful dignity—and smashed the padlock at a blow. Then all his followers, men, women and children, joined in an instant yell of triumph that scared the birds miles away. I know it made me jump; and as for the Fairy who lived in the Well, and had been very lonely lately, I have been told that it nearly frightened her into a fit.

Then they rushed for the Well and drank gallons of it—there was never so much water drunk in that parish before or since—and they went home in the highest glee. To hear the way they were laughing and shouting and singing, you would have thought it was whisky was in the Well. And the old priest himself

was flushed and triumphant, and after his late war-
like mood he was in the most boyish and tenderest
of tempers, and was beaming from ear to ear.

Now the Colonel was over at Castle Desmond
that morning, but there was the Devil to pay when
he came driving back past the Well on his car. I
am told that his rage was terrible. As ill-luck
would have it one of his farm-hands passed just then
with a cartload of manure, and the Colonel's first
words were an order to empty the cartload into
the Well. The fatal deed was done, and with a
shriek of despair—it was barely heard above the
splash of the manure—the Fairy fled from the
desecrated Well for ever.

So that was the end of the battle, and the Colonel
won a bitter victory. For when he grew calmer he
repented; "I beat them," he said to me, "but I'm
sorry I beat them that way; 'twas a mean trick."
And he lays the whole blame of it on Father
Flannery, and hates him for it; while the old priest
finds it hard to forgive Hercules for checkmating
him in the moment of his triumph by so unfair a
move.

Since then Father Peter has made no attempt to
lead his flock in mere worldly matters; he finds that
he has more than enough to do to try and lead them

on the way to Heaven, they are so laggard, says he, on that road, that, faith, you would think it was Hell he was trying to take them to.   He has seen so many vain struggles in his long life, for he can remember the days when O'Connell had Ireland on fire, and then his first task in Moher was to bury half his parishioners in one dead-pit at Liscannor in the Famine time; he can remember so many failures since, has christened and buried so many of his flock, has seen so much suffering in his desolate parish and yet so much happiness enjoyed in the teeth of Fortune, so many hopeful lives come to nothing, so many loud promises end in hopelessness, that now he has learnt Stoicism.

In those queer chatty sermons of his, when from his altar-step on the Sunday mornings he speaks with his people—often praising or rebuking them by name—he unconsciously teaches them a mournful philosophy, that this world is full of trouble and that it matters little what agonies a man finds on his pilgrimage if only he reaches the end of it with a clean heart.   Yet he is himself cheerful, though he has borne his full share of hardship.

If ever you visit Liscannor, if you see a dilapidated car driven by a ploughboy, and an old man—with a red jolly face—lounging on it (with the air of an emperor driving in a golden chariot) while the peasants salute him reverently and then grin widely as soon as his back is turned, you can thank your stars that for once you have seen a gentleman; for with all his faults, you might search a long while before finding a truer gentleman than the Colonel.

THE WHITE WITCH OF MOHER

ONCE as I was riding with Aileen Desmond along the road that runs northward towards Mount Elva from Moher, we passed a solitary cabin with grey thatch and green gables, and Aileen told me it was the home of Margaret McCaura, the "White Witch." A tall woman watched us from the door with grim eyes, but to tell the truth I took little heed of her for I was slave then to a daintier witchcraft. She had incredible powers—Aileen said—and people sought her from far corners of Ireland, she was honoured because her witchcraft was "white," was the gift of God or the Fairies, not the Devil's work, indeed the Moher folk thought her a saint; though she was very poor she took no payment from any one, she could cure any illness and tell strangers their past and future; but I had nothing wrong with me then—except lovesickness, and of that I did not want to be cured—I had not the least wish to know

"OLD CORNEY DESMOND"

my future sooner than I could help, and knew more than enough of my past.

Well, years afterwards, when Aileen was safe married, I was staying in Moher, and on one of my walks passed the cabin; it was roofless and the walls held only a tangle of brambles and nettles. Standing in that ruin, it was hard to believe that it had so recently been a place of pilgrimage. It must have been a wretched home, though it looked on a wide view of moors and sea with Castle Desmond's long battlements in the distance. I remember I had never been so struck by the fine look of the Castle; its big trees were like a green hillock against it, and there was a cloud of rooks over them, black specks drifting like scraps of burnt paper.

Then I grew curious about the White Witch and found I had missed knowing a wonderful woman. That hut had been her home all her life long, she was born and she died within those four walls; there, when she was no more than a girl, she came near dying of a brain-fever after a great trouble, and rose from her sick bed believing herself gifted with miraculous powers—a belief the country-side soon shared in those credulous days—there, during her long fame, thousands had come prying into their future with trembling hearts, people sick to death had been brought there to be healed.

I learnt all about her from Mick Doherty who in the days when he was sprightly was old Corney Desmond's servant and later was Shane's coachman, and now, bent and tottering, is rewarded for his faithfulness by an old age of comfort as keeper of the lodge at the Castle. My first memory of Mick shows him as a natty and sober fellow looking very dignified in an ancestral hat and a roomy old coat made for some swaggering flunkey. But that was when the lodge stood empty and the gate creaked on rusty hinges.

On my way back, that afternoon, one of his children, opening the gate for me, said that Mick was kept indoors by a cold, and as I saw this gave me a rare chance of questioning him I went into his home. The old man was pleased by my sympathy and seemed to be suffering only from laziness. He always patronises me; Shane and I are boys still to him although we are elderly, worse luck! and show necessary wrinkles. But his scorn for Shane's youthfulness does not overcome the reverence due to "one of the Family."

Mick welcomed me in his prim uncomfortable parlour. He sat in a stiff chair by the fireless grate, and I stood leaning my elbows on his mantelpiece. I heard the rooks cawing and through the window I could see the avenue winding under the trees. As he told me this story in his sing-song and plaintive brogue, the twilight was thickening, the trees were changing to black shadows, and darkness was coming down slowly over Moher.

This is a strange story and I have not much hope of bringing it home to you unless you know something of the old times in Ireland and the folk-lore of the Atlantic coast and unless you bear in mind that Corney's belief in the Witch's power was as full as her own. You should know too that the Desmonds are descended from that unruly house of Kildare— those dangerous Geraldines—and have the pride of their forefathers, so that there is a saying "as proud as the Devil or the Desmonds." Though scarcely fifteen years have gone since this happened, it is rightly a story of the old times, for Corney was one of the last of the old turbulent gentry and now you might search Ireland from sea to sea without finding a White Witch.

Corney Desmond had come near the end of his reckless life. Old and sick, outliving his friends and his time, harried by gout and harassed by creditors, he might well have found the end welcome; but he had a brute dread of death. He sat alone all day in the Tapestry Room at Castle Desmond. I know the room well, it is low and dark, with oak panelling partly hidden by tapestry showing a dim Apollo running after a faded nymph; on the left hand as you go in there is a huge canopied bed, and on the right a big chair—with the Desmond lion (nearly rubbed out now) blazoned on its peaked back, and with carved lions' heads on its handles—stands between the tiled fireplace and the deep window that looks out on the park and Moher Village and the long hulk of Mount Elva.

He sat there alone—nothing could make him keep his bed in the daytime, even when he was so weak that Mick Doherty had to carry him to the chair by the window—he let no one but Mick come near him, for he had so long been proud of his strength that now when he was broken he hated being seen, and refused to admit even his brother Hercules because Hercules was still flourishing. He spoke seldom and then as if his thoughts were running on old pleasures and old merry times with good fellows who had been long dead and forgotten. Now when by rights he should have been repenting the sins of his life—he was a passionate and fierce little man, and had been a terror to the godly—he was only sorry because they were over. A small bell stood on the round table by him, and Doherty never ventured near him except on the bell's summons.

"And well I remember the day," said Mick

Doherty, "seems like yestherday, though 'twas fifteen years, ay and more. It had been a soft mornin' an' a say-mist, but a wind came wid the turn o' the tide, an' the sun shone out. Misther Corney he sat in the big chair by the window; an' he stared out o' the window. When it was growin' late I was by him puttin' turf on the fire; but he niver noted me. 'Ah! Moher,' says he, 'ah! Moher, Moher! and must I be lavin' ye?'

"It stabbed me heart hearin' 'm. He was a good masther, so he was, barrin' when he was in a rage, though faith that was often. It was he that had the open hand and the warm heart.

"'Might I be makin' bould, your honour,' says I, 'but I'm heart-sore to see ye so poorly, an' mightn't I be afther callin' Docthor O'Donovan?'

"'No docthors for me,' says the masther, never lookin' away from the window; 'no damned docthors for me,' he said, savin' your presence, sir.

"'Humbly askin' your honour's pardon,' I says: I niver have durst go on spakin' to 'm but that his face was away from me—'may it plase your honour, the folk here do be sayin' there's an ould woman lives out yonther by Mount Elva—the White Witch they call her—an' she can cure annyone; she can nigh bring the dead to life. Ah, your honour,' says I, 'mightn't I be afther callin' Margaret McCaura?'

"Ould Corney he looks round at me terrible fierce; me heart stuck in me throat. 'Sure an' I meant no offence, your honour,' says I.

"The masther he looks back at the window. 'Margaret McCaura,' says he to himself twice. Then just as I was afther leavin' the room, 'Ay, Mick,' says he slow, 'ay, ye may be callin' her.'

"'Ah, now, thank ye kindly, your honour,' says I, 'in two twos I'll be bringin' her.'

"I went afther her like lightnin' for fear he'd be changin', an' sure enough he was ringin' for me afore I was off, but I wouldn't hear him. 'Twas mighty quiet out of doors; barrin' the crows that were makin' a great clatter in the park. In no time I got to her. She was sthandin' in the door of her house; she was that tall, her head touched the top of it. A dark smoky house 'twas. 'Twas quare entirely her livin' in it, wid folk offerin' her lashin's of gold. She had her hand up shadin' her eyes, for the sun was settin'. She looked mighty grave; she was always that.

"'I knew ye were comin',' she says. 'Misther Doherty, an' I know why too. It's Misther Desmond is dyin',' she says.

"'He is so, ma'am, the life is goin' quick out of him, God be good to him! I thought you'd be glad to be hearin' it.'

"'Glad?' she says, looking at me wid her eyes flamin'.

"'Ah! ma'am,' I cries, 'sure don't ye know well it's not that I'm manin'? Isn't it right, ma'am, you'd be sorry not to 've heard it, you that can save him?'

"'I'm comin',' she says, 'go back and tell him.' An' as I hurried back I remembered—God help me poor wits! it's wanderers they were always—that there was some ould sthory of Corney an' that same Margaret McCaura when they were youngsthers the both of them. He was a fine man was Corney, an' a divil wid the girls."

Then Doherty went on to say how he hurried back to the Castle, and had scarce reached the door before he saw the White Witch coming up the avenue under the trees, bearing herself proudly, she always walked like a queen; how when he opened the big door for her, she passed in, taking no more note of him than if he had been the dust under her feet, and how as she went up to the long hall towards the great staircase, you would have thought she owned Castle Desmond, till she reached the end of the hall and saw Corney's portrait hanging at the foot of the stairs—the portrait that shows him as a short and sturdy young squire, in a red hunting coat, and with a florid and bright face—then suddenly she stopped, throwing the shawl back off her head and staring up at the picture. Then he told me how as she went slowly up the wide staircase, she seemed much older, because she was walking with bent head and with her grey hair uncovered, and how when he showed her into the Tapestry Room she looked prouder than ever, but when she saw Corney sunk back in his chair—wrapped in an old dressing-gown, with his bandaged right leg propped on the deep window-sill —she turned as pale as lime.

Old Corney—said Mick Doherty—took no heed of her coming, but stared out of the window, breathing heavily with his mouth wide open; he had grown flabby and unwieldy, with his red under-hung face and shapeless lips—half hidden by his big white moustache—he had but little look of his portrait. Mick went from the room, and leaving the door ajar —the door faces the window—stood in the dark corridor watching them: he could see the Witch's profile, he said, as she stood at the table looking down at the sick man, her face looked terribly hard and was dark against the window, she held herself so stiffly that you would have thought she was the Desmond and he the McCaura; but Corney's face was still turned away. By this time, he said, the twilight was thickening, and the fire was beginning to redden the waxed floor and the tapestried walls. From Mick's place the wainscoted window must have been like a frame behind the two figures.

There was no sound but the cawing of the rooks. Then—

"May it plase your honour, sir," said the Witch in a shaky voice, "I do be hearin' that you're afther ordherin' me to come.'

"Orders!" said Corney slowly, "there is no question of orders between you and me, Margaret McCaura." He turned painfully towards her, leaning forward heavily on the left arm of his chair, with his gouty hand grasping the carved lion's head. He looked up at her, and his eyes, said Mick, were like the eyes of a wounded dog. She looked away from him.

"It's a long time since we met, and an ill change for both of us," he said. "I've been thinking a deal latterly of the old times. I was a bad friend to you, Margaret. You were a saint till I met you; ay, and the finest woman in Clare."

"Let bygones be bygones, Misther Desmond; 'tis small use pokin' white ashes. Let the past be. 'Tisn't for that you sent for me."

"You know well why I sent for you, Margaret; there's no one but you can help me. But I said to myself a hundred times that I would die rather than

F

ask you for anything. When I told Doherty he might call you I scarce knew what I was saying. He wasn't gone before I was ringing for him to come back, but he didn't hear me. I never humbled myself before. I'm old to begin now. But it's horrible to die. Don't mistake me, woman; I'd live my life over again just the same if I could. If I could! It's strange to grow old while your heart is as young as ever, to feel Death gripping you and stiffening you, while you are longing to be up and out with the boys. I'm in bitter need of help, Margaret."

"Listen to me. Cornalius Desmond," said the White Witch, turning to him and meeting his eyes. She spoke very quietly, her right hand was raised slightly ("So high," said Mick, putting his hand level with his steel watch-chain.) "Listen to me, Cornalius Desmond. When I was young I trusted ye. I niver knew how much I trusted ye till I found ye'd been foolin' me. Thrue I've been to ye all me life long. An' all the time I've hated the name of ye, an' the thought of ye, barrin' when I was seein' ye. Manny's the night I've laid awake cryin' to God to put black curses on ye. Manny's the time I've watched, wishful to curse ye as ye rode by, and when I saw ye from me window— you that had never a thought nor a look for me—

ridin' by gran' as if ye were the king of all Ireland, always me heart softened and went out to ye. 'Ah,' says I to meself, 'ah, an' hasn't he the right, a man like him, to fool all the women in the world?'

"And now ye're old, and ye're ugly and fat," (Corney winced) "but ye're as gran' to me as when ye were young. An' ye come cryin' to me for help. An' I hold your life in me hand. An' I'm shworn not to give it to ye.

"Listen to me. Years and years ago now I saw this day comin', ay, surely I did so. I saw ye dyin' in that same chair by that window. I knew that ye'd call me to save ye; an' that I'd have the power to save ye. An' I knew that seein' ye I'd forget iverythin' an' forgive iverythin', an' be clingin' to ye, an' be kissin' the feet of ye. An' I swore then that when this day came I'd never save ye. I swore it not once—ah, no! but a hundred times surely—by oaths 'twould be damnation to break—'twould be th' Unpardonable Sin—on the Sacrament, on God Himself.

"Death has hard hould of ye, now, Death and Hell. There's no repentance in ye. There are souls in Hell this minit that ye've sent there, an' they're cryin' out to God for the soul of ye. How could ye be in Heaven an' they tortured for iver an' iver?"

Corney was silent, breathing hard, purple in the

face, staring at her with dazed eyes. Suddenly the woman broke down; she fell on her knees by him., clutching his red swollen hand, she bowed her forehead on it. He sat looking down at her; he laid his right hand awkwardly on her grey hair.

"Lord knows," said Mick to me, "Lord knows how long they sthopped so, an' the fire shinin' on them. It seemed like a year, so it did. Terrible sthrange it looked; ye'd have thought they were young, the pair o' them, an' they so ould. Then the White Witch; she looks up, she grips the masther's two hands, ye'd have thought 'twas for her life she was beggin'.

"'Corney,' she whispers, so low that I could scarce hear her, 'Corney darlin', light o' me life, have mercy on yourself! Me soul is within ye, seven times dearer than me own soul y'are to me; gladly I'd burn in Hell for iver that you might be saved. Is it my forgiveness? Ah, what have I to forgive ye, pulse o' me heart! 'Tisn't too late, say but the word that you'll turn to God, an' I'll break me oaths for ye, I'll lose me soul for ye. Hell would be Heaven to me if you were saved, Corney.'

"'Woman,' says Misther Desmond, pantin', wrenchin' his hands away, and shovin' her from him. 'Woman, I'm too ould for preachin' at. I've

been a gentleman always. I've no shame of annythin' I've done. I'll niver ask forgiveness of man or
God.'

" He rings the bell by him, and falls back like a log
in his chair wid his eyes shut. 'Take the woman
away,' he says, 'for God's sake, Doherty, take her
away.'

" She sthands up, she looks at him for a minit, then
she dhraws her shawl over her head, an' she goes out
like a ghost. I hurried afther, and opened the hall
door for her. Lord! what a noise the crows were
makin'! the say-mist had come back, an' the night
had turned terrible cold. Then I went back to the
Tapestry Room; 'twas pitch dark if it hadn't been
for the fire that was blazin'. The masther, he hadn't
moved, an' the life was out of him."

THEIR LAST RACE

"WHEN I was a boy at Oriel," said my friend the Rector of Moher, "I thought it a fine thing to set myself on a pedestal and teach others how to behave. But now I'm not certain that my hearers don't know that way as well as myself."

We were walking along the Liscannor Road. The Reverend Cecil Lentaigne is small and sleek; he is short-sighted, and when he peers at you has a way of thrusting out his jaw as if he had an eye in his chin. He has a trim house and a granite church out on the Lisdoonvarna Road, and a very small congregation. No man could be more peaceful and his favourite study is the history of battles; none more prudish, and he knows Catullus and Villon by heart and loves the more passionate idylls of Theocritus. It is delightful to set him repeating the "In Nuptias Juliæ" and to note the lingering triumph of his voice when he reaches "Claudite ostia, virgines."

" So perhaps," he went on, " perhaps it's as well that I haven't risen in the Church, though I might choose a more cheerful parish. You come here from London and enjoy the wild scene and the solitude, but would you live here always? Why, man, after a year of it you'd be ready to sell your soul to be in an English country-side, and to see meadows with the wind driving a silver ripple over them instead of these moors, prosperous hedges instead of these ragged walls, and instead of these starved trees the oaks and the brooding sycamores."

The Rector delights in fine words; he loves to speak " like a book "—the book he once meant to write. Some laugh at him for it, but I own to much fellow-feeling with an honest prig. " Fancy,". he said, " fancy a man spending years in Oxford, loving every stone in the place, and then exiled to this Tanais. What is it Newman says? 'There used to be much snapdragon growing on the walls of Trinity.' Here it's on the thatched roofs that snapdragon grows. I'd change the brightest day here for the dullest in London when you pass thousands in the Strand, and don't know a soul, and feel as if you liked every one of them and would be glad to help them all if you could, a cheap charity when you know you can't help any one. Sure there's no place so homelike as London, with its Museum Read-

ing Room standing open for you, and the Gallery
where you can stare at some altar-piece, till you see
the Cathedral it came from, and smell the incense and
hear the monks droning in the choir and pass out of
the work-a-day world through the pointed gateway
of a triptych.

"To put a man like me to convert bog-trotters,
and wrangle with an illiterate boor like Flannery
(not that I ever do) is as bad as burning the bones
of the King of Edom for lime. Flannery's a kindly
old fellow, but his ignorance is appalling; he reads
nothing but his Breviary and if you talked to him
of Elia he'd think you meant Elias."

Here I missed some of his monologue, for I was
thinking of my friend Peter Flannery who is a boor
and whose long life has been one matter-of-course
self-sacrifice.

"And yet," said the Rector, "this countryside
should be a mine for a writer. As for Connemara,
across the bay yonder, why every glen of it has a
legend. Once I meant to write them, but that came
to nothing, like most of our hopes—dreams out of
the Ivory Gate and visions before midnight. I
remember I used to spend hours reading Carleton,
till I could fancy myself in the middle of a faction
fight, in the days before the Famine broke Ireland's
heart. It's all very well for you to laugh " (I had

turned away trying to hide a grin), "but every true Irishman would love a faction fight."

"Probably," I said, "your fancy for them is due to some remote ancestor."

"That hardly holds good since no ancestor of mine was a peasant," said he, flushing. "But about those Connemara legends, take that story now of the Dead Men's Race, don't you know it? I'm afraid it's too long to tell you."

However, it needed little persuading to make him tell it; he loves the music of his voice. I only wish I could have given it to you in his own words, for the story won greatly from its contrast with the teller.

I.—THE FACTION FIGHT.

In the heart of the Connemara Highlands, Carrala Valley hides in a triangle of mountains. Carrala Village lies in the corner of it towards Loch Ina, and Aughavanna in the corner nearest Kylemore. Aughavanna is a wreck now, if you were to look for it you would see only a cluster of walls grown over by ferns and nettles; but in those remote times, before the Great Famine, when no English was spoken in the Valley, there was no place more renowned for wild fun and fighting; and when its men were to be at a fair, every able-bodied fellow in the countryside took his "kippeen"—his cudgel—from its place in the chimney, and went out to do battle with a glad heart.

Long Mat Murnane was the king of Aughavanna.

There was no grander sight than Mat smashing his way through a forest of kippeens, with his enemies staggering back to the right and left of him ; there was no sweeter sound than his voice, clear as a bell, full of triumph and gladness, shouting, "Hurroo! whoop! Augha-vanna for ever!" Where

"LONG MAT MURNANE"

his kippeen flickered in the air his followers charged after, and the enemy rushed to meet him, for it was an honour to take a broken head from him.

But Carrala Fair was the black day for him. That

day Carrala swarmed with men—fishers from the
near coast, dwellers in lonely huts by the black
lakes, or in tiny ragged villages under the shadow of
the mountains, or in cabins on the hill-sides—every
little town for miles, by river or sea-shore or moun-
tain-built, was emptied. The fame of the Aughavanna men was their ruin, for they were known to
fight so well that every one was dying to fight them.
The Joyces sided against them; Black Michael
Joyce had a farm in the third corner of the Valley,
just where the road through the bog from Aughavanna (the road with the cross by it) meets the highroad to Leenane, so his kin mustered in force. Now
Black Michael, "Meehul Dhu," was Long Mat's
rival; though smaller he was near as deadly in fight,
and in dancing no man could touch him, for it was
said he could jump a yard into the air and kick himself behind with his heels in doing it.

The business of the Fair had been hurried so as to
leave the more time for the pleasure, and by five of
the afternoon every man was mad for the battle.
Why, you could scarcely have moved in Callanan's
Field out beyond the churchyard at the end of the
Village, it was so packed with men—more than five
hundred were there; and you could not have heard
yourself speak, for they were jumping and dancing,
tossing their caubeens, and shouting themselves

hoarse and deaf—"Hurroo for Carrala!" "Whoop
for Aughavanna!" Around them a mob of women,
old men and children, looked on breathlessly. It
was dull weather, and the mists had crept half way
down the dark mountain walls, as if to have a nearer
look at the fight.

As the chapel clock struck five, Long Mat Murnane gave the signal. Down the Village he came,
rejoicing in his strength, out between the two last
houses, past the churchyard and into Callanan's
Field; he looked every inch a king; his kippeen
was ready, his frieze coat was off, with his left hand
he trailed it behind him holding it by the sleeve,
while with a great voice he shouted—in Irish—
"Where's the Carrala man that dare touch my
coat? Where's the cowardly scoundrel that dare look
crooked at it?"

In a moment Black Michael Joyce was trailing his
own coat behind him, and rushed forward with a
mighty cry, "Where's the face of a trembling Aughavanna man?" In a moment their kippeens clashed;
in another, hundreds of kippeens crashed together,
and the grandest fight ever fought in Connemara
raged over Callanan's Field. After the first roar of
defiance the men had to keep their breath for the
hitting; so the shout of triumph and the groan as

one fell were the only sounds that broke the music
of the kippeens clashing and clicking on one another,
or striking home with a thud.

Never was Long Mat nobler, he rushed ravaging
through the enemy, shattering their ranks and their
heads, no man could withstand him; Red Callanan
of Carrala went down before him; he knocked the
five senses out of Dan O'Shaughran of Earrennamore,
that herded many pigs by the sedgy banks of the
Owen Erriff; he hollowed the left eye out of Larry
Mulcahy, that lived on the Devil's Mother Mountain
—never again did Larry set the two eyes of him on
his high mountain-cradle; he killed Black Michael
Joyce by a beautiful swooping blow on the side of the
head—who would have dreamt that Black Michael
had so thin a skull?

For near an hour Mat triumphed, then suddenly
he went down under foot. At first he was missed
only by those nearest him, and they took it for
granted that he was up again and fighting. But
when the Aughavanna men found themselves out-
numbered and driven back to the Village, a great
fear came on them; for they knew that all Ireland
could not outnumber them if Mat was to the fore.
Then disaster and rout took them, and they were
forced backwards up the street, struggling desperately
till hardly a man of them could stand. And when

the victors were shouting themselves dumb and
drinking themselves blind, the beaten men looked for
their leader.   Long Mat was prone; his forehead was
smashed, his face had been trampled into the mud—
he had done with fighting.   His death was untimely,
yet he fell as he would have chosen—in a friendly
battle.   For when a man falls under the hand of an
enemy (as of any one who differs from him in creed
or politics) revenge and black blood live after him;
but he who takes his death from the kindly hand of
a friend leaves behind him no ill-will but only gentle
regret for the mishap.

II.—By the Black Cross.

That night Carrala Village was as quiet as the
dead; but in the other two corners of the Valley only
the dead had quiet.   For in Joyce's Farm and in
Aughavanna the boys were waking Long Mat and
Black Michael.   Outside Murnane's cabin, women
knelt raising the "keen," that cry like the sea-wind
in the mountains when a storm is beginning.   Indoors
the dead man lay in his shroud on the table, with
candles at his head and feet.   Margaret Murnane,
the widow, stood by him, welcoming all comers.
Each who came took her by the hand, saying, "I'm
sorry for your loss, ma'am"; she answered each, "I

thank you kindly." Her eyes were tearless; she was very quiet and showed no sorrow. The men wondered that she should mind so little; they sat round the table and drank the plentiful whisky, talking at first in hushed tones of the dead man, then they grew merry talking of his merry doings, till soon Aughavanna rang with their songs and their laughing.

Then Margaret slipped out past the keening women—they looked ghastly in the yellow light from the open door—and she hurried along the road through the bog to the Leenane highroad. It was a grey moonless night; the mists had come down from the mountains and filled the Valley. She hardly knew where she was going, felt she must get to a quiet place, the noise was killing her. She could not believe it was her man they were waking; surely it was years since they brought him home dead; he had been all she had in the world, a loving and kind man to her.

At length the sound of the singing and keening died behind her, so she went more slowly. Then suddenly the wind brought an echo of singing and wailing from in front of her. She stopped with her hand on her heart; thought the Mountain Spirits were mocking her misery. Then she remembered that at the Farm the Joyces were waking Black Michael.

Now she knew where she was hurrying, for she saw the big black cross by the wayside. She knelt on the stones by it, tried to pray, could not remember a word, her throat and her eyes were burning; she flung her arms round the rough wood of the cross and lay at its foot.

She never knew how long she lay there before she heard a girl coming down the road, sobbing and crying aloud. The girl stopped with a cry of terror. "Holy Mother of God!" she said in a trembling voice, "what's that?" Margaret got up, leaning her right hand on the cross.

"In the Lord's Name, who are you at all at all?" cried the girl. "Is it a living woman you are?"

As she spoke her shawl fell, and Margaret knew her for Kitty Joyce, the girl that was to have married Black Michael. Kitty knew her too.

"Is it you?" she cried. "Oh! woman, woman, what right have you here? And you that are wife to a murderer!"

But Margaret Murnane stretched out open arms to her; the girl shrank back, putting out her hands to keep Margaret off. For a moment their eyes met; then the girl laid her head on the widow's heart.

III.—THEIR LAST RACE.

When the dead had been duly waked for two days
and nights, the burying day came. All the morning
Long Mat Murnane's coffin lay on four chairs by his
cabin, with a kneeling ring of dishevelled women
keening round it. Every soul in Aughavanna and
their kith and kin had gathered to do him honour.
And when the Angelus bell rang across the Valley
from the chapel, the mourners fell into ranks, the
coffin was lifted on the rough hearse, and the motley
funeral—a line of carts with a mob of peasants
behind, a few riding, but most of them on foot—
moved slowly towards Carrala. The women were
crying bitterly, keening like an Atlantic gale; the
men looked as sober as if they had never heard of a
wake, and spoke sadly of the dead man, and of what
a pity it was that he could not see his funeral.

The Joyces, too, had waited, as was the custom,
for the Angelus bell; and now Black Michael's funeral
was moving slowly towards Carrala along the other
side of the bog. Before long, either party could
hear the keening of the other, for you know the
roads grow nearer as they converge on Carrala.
Before long either party began to fear that the other
would be there first.

There is no knowing how it happened, but the

funerals began to go quicker, keeping abreast; then still quicker, till the women had to break into a trot to keep up; then still quicker, till the donkeys were galloping, and till every one raced at full speed, and the rival parties broke into a wild shout of "Aughavanna abu!" "Meehul Dhu for ever!"

For the dead men were racing—feet foremost—to the grave; they were rivals even in death. Never did the world see such a race, never was there such whooping and shouting. Where the roads meet in Callanan's Field the hearses were abreast; neck to neck they dashed across the trampled fighting-place, while the coffins jogged and jolted as if the two dead men were struggling to get out and lead the rush; neck to neck they reached the churchyard, and jammed in the gate. Behind them the carts crashed into one another, and the mourners shouted as if they were mad.

But the quick wit of the Aughavanna men triumphed; for they seized their long coffin and dragged it in, and Long Mat Murnane won his last race. The shout they gave then deafened the echo up in the mountains, so that it has never been the same since. The victors wrung one another's hands; they hugged one another.

"Himself would be proud," they cried, "if he hadn't been dead!"

THE SNIPE'S LUCK

THE Rector was beaming placidly at the fire; that last glass of port had perceptibly increased his benevolence. His blonde hair shone in the firelight and there was a delicate flush on his face; he looked like a boy of twenty. He was a pleasant sight, he was so happy and sleek. We were sitting by the big fireplace in the dining-room at Castle Desmond; Madden the Agent,

"A MOONLIGHTER"

Colonel Hercules Desmond were with us.

"Surely," he said to me, " nothing is so lovely as those pennons of flame, 'banners yellow, glorious golden;' as Catullus wrote, 'aureas quatiunt comas.

As a lover of Hawthorne and Hazlitt I boast myself of the brotherhood of fireworshippers, and want no meaner travels while I can watch a sinking fire and explore the caverns of enchantment in that miniature sunset." Plainly he was in one of his wordy moods.

"But as I was saying," said the Colonel in a louder voice — for he hates any side-talk while he is speaking—"as I was saying, we pay nowadays for their fun ; if we're beggars, it's because our fathers went on as if they were kings, bad luck to them ! and their pictures on the walls there see us stinting and pinching to make up for the money they wasted at yonder table.   Many's the hundred of pounds that has been squandered in this dining-room.   That's all over now, more's the pity.   There's been no harder luck in the world than the luck of the Irish landlords, —crushed by the debts of others, robbed of our rents, and betrayed by each English party in turn, and if we're murdered, it's for the sins of our fathers. Begad, Rector, it's not often I quote the Scripture."

"Ah, yes ! " said the Rector, glad to get another word in :

> " 'They say the Lion and the Lizard keep
>   The Courts where Jamshyd gloried and drank deep.'

or as Browne has it : 'The iniquity of oblivion

blindly scattereth her poppy and deals with the memory of man without distinction to merit of perpetuity.' ''

Colonel Desmond flushed ; he dislikes having texts thrown at him.

'' Browne ? '' said the Agent—a long lean man with a dreary and gentle face—'' Browne ? was that one of the Kenmare people now ? ''

'' Kenmare ? '' said the Colonel, '' and begad, that's a worse district than Moher. It's lncky for you, sir, you're not agent there now ; if you were you'd have been dead long ago, though they do call you 'The Snipe.' Did I ever tell you, Lentaigne, how I introduced Mr. Madden here to young Lady Kilkee ? a foolish, wool-gathering little doll she is, and always talks to you as if she was thinking of something miles away. I told her I was going to bring her the famous agent that was known as ' the Snipe,' because half Clare had tried a shot at him. So I introduced him. ' How d'ye do, Mr. Snipe,' says she. Upon my soul ! they're a nice couple those Kilkees. That young Kilkee is as cold as a fish, and wouldn't trouble to speak to the Queen. The last time he dined here he never opened his mouth.''

The Rector was going to speak ; I saw a quotation in his eye, and doubted whether the Colonel could stand another, so I broke in.

"Now, Mr. Madden, what was the narrowest escape you ever had?"

"The narrowest? Begad, 'twas the time he tried to get me shot instead of himself."

"Don't mind the Colonel now. It's joking he is. Not but that it was a near thing. But it's an old story."

"Never mind that, Mr. Madden, sir. An old story is old wine," said the Colonel (by-the-by, he is always strangely polite to the agent because he considers him 'an inferior'; rudeness from him is a compliment, for it implies that he thinks you an equal, and that means that he thinks a great deal of you).

The Agent began drearily, apparently addressing the fire.

"'Twas when Mr. Desmond was at school that I evicted old Catherine McCaura. She never paid a penny rent in her life and ye'd have thought her cabin was a pig-stye. The poor-house was the right place for her; but she wouldn't go. And of course she made a scene. I had to have her dragged out of the hut screaming; then she knelt in the mud and caught me round the knees, and when they cut the ropes holding on the thatched roof ye'd have thought it was her throat was being cut. And half the country-side was looking on, cursing me for my 'cruelty,' save the mark!

" Still she wouldn't go to the House, nor to her neighbours', and that night she went back and slept on the bare earth of her cabin, though there was no roof nor door, and 'twas raining in floods. She was dead in a week, and of course they said I murdered her.

" Well, she had been dead three or four days, when one evening I was driving here to the Castle from the Fair at Ennistimon. I'd met the Colonel at the Fair, and knew he was coming home along the same road not more than a mile behind me, lucky 'twas for me ! and I was about a half-mile from the Liscannor Cross-roads. Precious cold it was, and a salt wind was blowing right in my face. That old brown mare of mine has a way of shying at every heap of stones by the wayside if they're shiny after rain."

" And I had a horse once that did that same."

" Is that a fact now, Colonel ? Well, what with one thing and another 'twas a dull drive, and none the pleasanter from knowing that every shadow might be a Moonlighter. Ye haven't an idea how many shadows there are by a road at night till ye've been shot at once or twice. Of course I'd my loaded revolvers. But I am a peaceful man, and was more afraid of them than of the Moonlighters."

" Afraid ? Don't mind him, now, there's no braver

man in Clare. Not that revolvers are much good.
I tell you they're more afraid of my stick than of all
Shane's artillery. If you met Shane driving you'd
think he was a battery in disguise, a masked battery,
begad. But that boy overdoes everything. Look at
the way he shakes hands; I'd rather shake hands
with a bear any day." He looked pityingly at his
red, gouty hand.

"Is that a fact now? Well, I was a short half-
mile from the Cross-roads when suddenly I saw a
light under the trees. 'Twas only a spark, but 'twas
more than enough; for why should any one be there
at that hour, and Dark Andy dead? I stopped the
horse, and I watched. The light went out, then I
saw it again, 'twas no bigger than a pin's head, then
it went out again.

"'Heaven save us!' said John, my man, 'that's
where Dark Andy's ghost walks, 'tis he!' 'Faith, I
wish 'twas,' says I, 'for the old man 'd make a harmless ghost. But I never heard of a ghost smoking a
pipe yet.' I knew there was some man in the field,
at the side of the wall, stooping lighting a pipe, and
what did he want at this side of the wall? 'Twas
me he wanted. And I can tell ye I thanked my
stars that the Colonel was behind me. But I'd have
thanked them more if he'd been in front.

"I waited about quarter of an hour, it seemed like

a year, and the mare, bad luck to her! wouldn't
stand easy. I stared at the Cross-roads till my eyes
were sore and starting out of my head. But I could
see nothing but the black lump of trees.

"Then at last the Colonel came up with me. 'What's
the matter, Mr. Madden?' says he. He laughed
as if 'twas the grandest joke. 'An' if there was,'
says he, 'what sin is there in lighting a pipe?'"

"Begad, I was half asleep myself, so I thought
you were dreaming."

"'Drive on Pat,' says he to his boy, and his side-
car passed me. I whipped up my horse close after
him. I was afraid, sure enough, but 'twas too soon
to own it. Perhaps I was wrong, and anyway the
Colonel was an army in himself. Nothing more
could I see. 'I've been making a hare of myself,'
thought I, but I'd my revolver ready.

"There wasn't a sound but the wheels and hoofs
and the wind in the trees. 'Tis wonderful the noise
those trees make at night. The road under them
was pitch black, and the Colonel's car disappeared
into it like into a tunnel.

"That minute came a shout, 'Sthand.' It sent
the blood out of me; and a man with a lanthorn
jumped into the road. By the light I could see him
holding the Colonel's horse; he had a handkerchief
round his face, and behind him were half a dozen

fellows with guns. ' Don't sthir a finger,' he shouts
at the Colonel (thinking it was me, and glad I was
that it wasn't). The Colonel jumps to his feet,
standing on the lip of the car.

" ' What's this mean ? ' he roars, ' what the Hell
does this mean ? '

" Faith, sir, I didn't think any living man had such
a loud voice.

" ' Gracious Powers ! ' cried the man jumping back
as if he was shot. ' Gracious Powers ! 'tis ould
Herc'les ! ' and in a second the place was pitch
dark, and in a minute there wasn't a man within a
mile of us. "

The Rector had his eyeglasses up and was benignly
studying the agent; but just then Madden turned
to him, and he dropped them nervously. The Rector
shrinks from looking any one in the face through
his glasses, as if that would show an unmannerly
curiosity. Speaking to you he will look at you
blandly and vainly with his short-sighted eyes; but
as soon as your head is turned, he will study you
through his glasses.

" Upon my word, Colonel," he said, " you seem to
be a terror to evil-doers."

" Sir," with a pleased smile, " I am a terror to
any one who meddles with me."

"And they left no trace but two empty whisky bottles," said the agent. "They had whisky and pipes to pass away the time pleasantly while waiting for me. But for that and the wind blowing in my face, I'd not be here now. I'd swear McCaura was their leader."

"Those McCauras," said the Rector, "are a black unreasonable brood. Though for that matter, there is no stiffer-necked race in Ireland than the Clare peasantry."

"I disagree with you entirely," said the Colonel, "there's no kindlier people in the world. Why, I remember the days when there wasn't a boy in Moher wouldn't have died for the Desmonds, and if they're readier now to kill us than to die for us, it's the fault of the agitators."

"The old loyalty to the landlord," said the Rector, "is dead with the old sympathy. Nowadays the landlords are growing more and more English; the peasants are growing more and more American."

"For my part," said the Agent, "I think that the peasants' worst enemies are the village shopkeepers who deliberately let them run into debt to secure their custom and to get the whip-hand of them."

"Anyway, that was a narrow escape," said the Colonel; "Mr. Madden, you've always wonderful luck; now that might have happened to a man a hundred

times, and he never escape once. Did y'ever hear
tell how they killed Callanan's herd?" and he began
a long-winded yarn. I missed it, staring at the
Agent's mild face, thinking of the hatred he had
earned, yet I always found him kindly enough, and
have heard that though his wife was a bitter shrew
he bore patiently with her, and was a long-suffering
father.

He was speaking again. "You're right, Mr.
Lentaigne, to call them unreasonable. It's wonderful
to hear their unreasonable reasoning when you ask
for the rent; often I end by believing them while
I'm sure they're lying. And can't they see that if I
evict them it's not for my pleasure? Why should
they stop on the land if they won't pay? And if
the landlord wants the rent, what am I to do? My
business is to make them pay what they owe,
and they hate me for it—as they say—'like black
hell.'"

"Well," said the Rector, in his most musical tones,
"I sympathise with them in that."

"Upon my soul! I take it very kindly of ye
sir!"

"Do not misapprehend me, Mr. Madden, I love
to think there is no man so far below me or above
me, but I can feel with him; my heart goes out alike
to that wild rackety poet, "Né de Paris emprés

"I BELIEVE THEM WHILE I'M SURE THEY'RE LYING"

Ponthoise,' or to the doings of Francis, 'mirabil vita del poverel di Dio;' to the drunken squireen boosing in his old crumbling house, to the worn peasant-woman staggering under the creel of turf, to the evicting landlord or the Moonlighter; so, too, I can long for perilous travel and cry with that divine 'Song of Joys':

> 'Oh to sail to sea in a ship!
> To leave this steady, unendurable land,'

though I am a miserable sailor."

"Begad, Lentaigne," said the Colonel, " I think y' ought to be fined every time you quote Scripture. Not that I'm saying anything against the Song of Songs."

In the interest of peace I again broke in, " It's too much to expect outsiders to understand Irishmen; but it would be a blessed thing if only we could understand one another. Now in this everlasting Land question, the fact is there's a deal to be said on both sides."

Said the Colonel, " I disagree with you entirely."

H

AT THE RISING OF THE MOON

PARADISE Walk, in Chelsea, is a slum close to big
houses. In the day-time it is quiet enough, but
to know what life there means you should see it
at night. Last Saturday afternoon I met a friend,
an Irish curate.

"D'ye know," said he, "that there's a Clare man,
McCarthy his name is, dying in Johnson's house in
Paradise Walk? You might do worse now than go
and see him. He'd be right glad to see any one who
knows County Clare, and I've little time to give him
myself."

Well, as my hands were free then, I strolled down
to the slum. The man who christened it had a fine
sense of humour.

I found McCarthy in a cellar lit only by a dirty
skylight. He was lying on a mattress with a heap
of rags over him for bed-clothes. A small girl was
with him; he was talking to her in a monotonous

voice like a man in a fever. She was not listening, I think, and soon after I came she slipped out. It was easy to see that he had nearly done with life.

"From th' ould counthry, sir?" he said, in a weak voice. "Sir, ye're kindly welcome."

I took a seat by him, a rickety chair.

"Yes, sir, McCaura me name is—Michael McCaura from Moher. McCarthy they call me here. An' ye know Moher? 'Tis a weary long way from here."

Then suddenly I remembered him, this was Michael McCaura, who used to live hard by the Liscannor bog, about a mile from the sea, half a farmer and half a fisherman. He lived in a little mean cabin by the wayside; it was built roughly of stone, and long grass and snapdragon flourished on its thatched roof. When I was staying at Castle Desmond, he was pointed out to me as a dangerous man, a Moonlighter and a ringleader in mischief. He looked much older now, and was broken by sickness.

"A crule long way," he went on. "Ah! what wouldn't I give to be there now, thrampin' along the Liscannor road, leadin' th' ould mare wid the cart creakin' behind her, past the fields where the girls are sthoopin' diggin' the pitaties, an the farms where ivery livin' soul has a kind look for ye, an' a kind

word; an' the dogs themselves—faith, an' the pigs
too—are glad to see ye as ye go by.   What wouldn't
I give to dhrive int' Ennistimon Fair in the raw of
the morn, wid all the cattle lowin', an' all the fowls
clutherin', an' all the pigs, the craythurs, gruntin', an'

"LEADIN' TH' OULD MARE"

all the small boneens squealin' as if they were kilt.
But I'm past prayin' for."

I was hardly listening to him.   In the room overhead there were shrieks and curses.   Johnson, the
cabman, was drunk, and was jumping on his wife.
Nobody interfered with him, it was nobody's business,
the woman was used to it.

I asked McCaura why he left Moher.

" Is it why I left Moher, sir? There's no need o' hidin' 't now, little can annyone harm me. I'm beyond throublin'. An' did y'iver hear tell of Healy's Farm, sir ? "

Then at once I was all ears, for every one in Ireland—from Malin Head to Mizen Head—knows of the grim fight at Healy's Farm out by Lisdoonvarna in Clare.

" 'Tis a long sthory, sir, an' 'tis aisy to blame 's—when did a gentleman iver understhand 's ?—'tisn't in Nature. When I was a lad ould Corney Desmond —bless 'm, 'twas he was the good landlord, so he was —ould Corney, he dies. Then the Shnipe—th' agent from Ennis—an' a crule scoundrel—he managed th' estate. We hated him like Hell, he was harder than rock, but the Divil keeps his own, an' we could never kill him once annyhow. For, mind ye, down Moher way we're men ; an' 'tis bad to meddle wid us.

" Look ye, sir, we were poorer than the dead ; manny and manny a . day we hadn't a taste of mate, only pitaties, an' rotten ones often. Why, th' acre couldn't keep the life in 's, much less pay the rent. Then comes th' agent—' Pay the rent,' says he. ' An' how can we, when we haven't 't ?' says we.

' Ye have 't, or if ye haven't 't y' ought to have 't,' says he. ' Pay 't, or out ye go,' says he.

"Ah! what's the good of tellin' y' all this? Haven't ye heard it a thousand times? an' did y' iver believe 't? 'Tis God's truth for all that. An', of course, we'd our Secret Society; where isn't it in Ireland? —an' glad I was to be of 't, an' mebbe ye'd have been that same. We'd our oaths an' our meetin's, an' our long thramps by night, warnin' them that harmed us; an' if they wouldn't be warned—we sthopped 'm.

" Listen to me, man—sir, I mane—what else could we do? Would ye have us lie an' be thrampled on an' stharved, an' we that owned the lan' by rights as our fathers did in th' ould times, hunthreds an' hunthreds of years ago. If we McCauras had our rights wouldn't we own the counthry of the Clan Caura, half Munsther 'tis?

" An' 'twasn't the landlords we were agin most, sure they were born so, an' could they help themselves? 'Twas agin them that should 've been wid us an' bethrayed us. If all the tenants in Ireland sthood shouldther to shouldther we'd 've had our rights ages ago. But did they? Warn't there in ivery parish the bodaghs, that for their own comfort wint agin the cause, an' took th' impty farms? So we warned 'm, we frighted 'm, we burnt their crops, we kilt their cattle—we bet 'm, we shot 'm in the legs, an' if that wouldn't tache 'm—why we did what had to be done.

"Listen to me, man, 'twas no fool's playin' wid us, 'twas life an' death wid us.

"What's that ye say? Is't why did we hurt the cattle? An' did we want to hurt 'm, the craythurs? Wasn't it the men that owned 'm that we hurt through 'm? An' for that matter why would anny man be shootin' a landlord if he didn't desarve it? an' if he desarved 't wasn't it just?

"Years ago now—I disremember how manny, 'twas six I think—Maddigan he comes' to Moher. Soon he knew ivery one, he'd a sootherin' way wid him, an' was always at the shebeen. Then he was shworn into the Society, made believe to be a pathriot, a brave man an' thrue, said he was hidin' from the polis an' 'twas he shot Scully's agent down yonther at Cahir. An' said he was a Fenian Centre, an' the night was near, when in ivery parish in Ireland the boys would gather at the Risin' o' the Moon, to sthrike a blow for th' Ould Counthry, an' she be free at last, and we have our right agin.

"Proud we were of 'm, an' afore the year was out 'twas he was head of iverythin'—ah! but 'twas he was the gran' spaker. He planned iverythin' an' ordered iverythin'; we trusted an' followed him like dogs, an' why not?

" Then in the winther time, says he, 'That Healy that lives out behind Lisdoonvarna yonther, he's a curse to the counthy, wid 's land-grabbin' an' 's spyin',' says he. 'By this an' by that he's goin' a dale too far, I'm thinkin', but we'll tache 'm a lesson. We'll make an example of 'm,' says he.

" 'Tis we were glad enough, we were spoilin' for a job an' not one of 's like Healy. Then says Maddigan, 'Healy's a stubborn dog, an' to fright 'm proper we'll show 'm how manny of 's there are; sorra a one that's here to-night must miss 't; we'll all go, an' 'tis all the betther batin' he'll git if he don't swear th' oath.'

" So on the Thursday we met at the Risin' o' the Moon in the field by the bog behind Healy's Farm; near ivery man of 's. There was big Dan Cassidy, of Kilfenora, the biggest man in Clare; there was John Lonergan and Michael Lonergan, of Liscannor, them that owned th' ould hooker, own brothers they were; Ronan, of Kilfenora, that was Larry Ronan's cousin, an' little Pat O'Brien an' Shaughnessy, of Lahinch, 'twas Pat that kilt Callanan's herd—poor Pat was a dead man that night, God be good to 'm— miles some of 'm came, the bravest boys in the counthry-side; then there was Maddigan an' meself.

" Th' eight of 's were waitin', an' a bitter shiverin' night 'twas, an' wet unther-foot, when the moon began showin' behind the Burren hills in a mist, wid a cryin' face on her. An' ivery man of 's had crape tied round his face, an' had a gun. Mind ye, man, we'd no heart to kill the craythur, 'twas frightin' 'm we were afther; an' half them the boys kilt, were kilt by accident; whose fault was 't if a man was that wake that one polthogue over the head wid a sthick or a shot in the leg 'd be the death of 'm? A man that wake oughtn't to be let live. Not but that I'm wake enough meself now.

"HE KNOCKS AT THE DOOR"

"His gate was open, an' we crep' up the path to the door one after th' other, no man spakin'. I was last but one, an' I thought some'at was wrong, 'twas so dead quiet an' the dog niver barked. There was a light inside, we saw 't through the chink round the shutther, but 'twas sthrange the shutther was up.

"Cassidy, he thumps on the door wid his fist; sorra an answer, he knocks agin.

"'Who's there?' cries Healy, 'who's there now, annyhow?'

"''Tis the polis,' says Cassidy.

"'The polis is 't?' says Healy, 'an' what d'ye want now at this hour o' the night? Wait a minit, will ye?'

"Then I heard shufflin' about inside; thought I, he's getthin' out o' bed. Then he opens the door a weeshy bit; an' Cassidy he dashes it wide wid his shouldther, an' we rushes into the house.

"We weren't in 't afore we heard Nolan, the head consthable—he'd a voice clare an' sthrong like a thrumpet—shout, 'Surrenther in the name o' the Queen!' an' we saw the room full of polis; an' that minit they sprang at us.

"'We're thrapped! by God!' cries Cassidy, an' a big consthable was on me.

"Niver did ye hear such a scrimmage, thramplin' an' wrastlin', an' smashin' wid butts or sthicks or chairs, or annythin' we could lay hould on, but not a shot fired, for divil a bit could annyone aim at annyone.

"An' all the time Mrs. Healy—a little grey woman she is, wid a face like a sthone—she sthands sthill by the scrimmage, holdin' a candle up as high as she could for us to see to kill one another by.

"I felled one man an' bruk from another, an' because I was nearest the door I made a bolt for 't, an' was yond the gate afore ye could spake. Then I sthopped to see if I could help the boys anny, though they were done for. All roun' I heard whistles, an' consthables runnin' up.

"An' I crouched at the far side of the wall. Inside the frame o' the door I could see the room wid ivery one all in a black lump fightin' like divils, an' the yellow light round 'm an' 'tween their legs.

"Then two came swingin' an' reelin' out o' the house. 'Twas Cassidy thryin' to git free an' Nolan houldin' 'm; they were gran' men both, mighty an' sthrong. They were grapplin' an' wrastlin' for dear life, sthrugglin' wid naked han's. Nolan had revolvers in 's belt, but he didn't use 'm; perhaps couldn't, or perhaps wanted to fight it fair, man to man.

"Cassidy was the sthronger, but Nolan he held 'm like grim death—he was a brave man.

"They came on sthaggerin' an' shwayin' an' shlippin' in the mud unther-foot till they weren't a yard from me. Then they sthopped in a death grip, swingin' roun' an' roun', gaspin' an' sobbin'. They were so locked I couldn't tell which was which, but when the light caught Nolan's revolvers. Of a sudden one was done—'twas Nolan—he shlipped, and Cassidy heaved 'm clane off 's feet an' then swang 'm down, hurled 'm down, smashin' 's head agin the sthone wall.

"I heard his head smash, it sounded like a broken keg, it made me blood cold.

"Nolan he makes one shrug to git up. 'Holy Mother o' God!' he cries, in a wake child's whisper, then he falls flat, like a log.

"Ay, his head sounded like a broken keg, it made me heart sick.

"Did y' iver hear tell how we shmuggled kegs o' potheen by the Cliffs o' Moher—'twas brought by hookers across the bay from Connemara—the polis niver caught 's though they ran 's hard. Once when Father Doherty, of Corrofin, was a sthranger there-abouts—an' a fine upsthandin' man he is, wid a kind heart of 's own, God bless 'm—he comes up the rocks to our shebeen, an' he asks for a sup. Sure we gave 't to 'm wid a heart an' a half—for when did a priest bethray us? 'Then,' says he, sudden, 'so I have ye at last, me fine boys. I'm no priest,' says he, 'I'm an Inspecthor in disguise,' says he. 'Twas only his joke, ye know, but faith 'twas near bein' a wry joke for him—for a thraneen we'd 've thrown 'm over the Cliffs, we were mad wid 'm for thrappin' 's at last by sich a coward's thrick. He laughed on th' other side of 's face when he saw what we were afther, an' turned whiter than whitewash. 'For

God's sake be aisy, boys! don't ye see it's jokin' I am,' says he.

"But that's neither here nor there.

"What's that ye say, sir? About Healy's Farm?

"Nolan he lay as sthill as a sthone, the life was out of 'm. Cassidy never looked twice at 'm, an' was past me like a flash. I was off, too, across the bog; lightnin' was slow to me, till I sat by Larry Ronan's hearth. He's a soft man is Larry, that has no stomach for fightin', but he was game to swear that I spent the night wid him, then how could the polis harm me?

"Next mornin', puttin' a bould face on it, I went into Lisdoonvarna to see the poor boys marched off. One by one they came by, ivery man of 'm (barrin' Cassidy, and me, and poor Pat that was lyin' dead in the farm, God rest his soul!) wid the darbies on, an' aich wid two polis to kape 'm, an' the mounted polis ridin' afore an' behind. It wanted an army to hould 'm. They walked wid proud faces an' a laughin' word for the folk; and 'twas manny that ran out an' grasped 'm by the hand.

"Maddigan was wid 'm, but when I saw 'm I knew 't all: he looked no man in the face, he was 'fraid o' the crowd, an' why was he that? Ye see, man, 'twas a thrap, a cursed thrap. Maddigan he was a thraitor, he never shot a man in 's life, the coward!

He was no pathriot, but an informer, an' all the time he was foolin' 's. May black disthruction rot 'm! God forgive me for sayin' 't, I mane may God give 'm what he desarves!

"I'd have kilt 'm then if I'd had the chance; but he was safe from me—there was no reachin' 'm. But 'twas all up wid me if he played informer, for if once the polis have hould o' ye 'tis hard but they hang ye somehow, though 'tis for murtherin' the wrong man, one ye never laid eyes on, much less a finger.

"So afore the week was out I was here in London. An' that's why I left Moher, an' bitterly I rued 't; manny's the heart-scaldin' I've had of 't.

"Ah! what wouldn't I give to smell the say agin, an' be fishin' in my corracle out unther the Cliffs wid the rollers rockin' me, an' feel the fish flutherin'; or sthandin' out to th' open say in Lonergan's ould hooker, an' she shiverin' unther ye an' slidtherin' over the wather wid her mast creakin', and wid the wather sparklin' like fish an' purrin' roun' her bows as if 'twas glad to feel th' ould boat on 't agin, an' th' islands on the right o' ye—-Innismaan, Innishere an' Arranmore—an' the Connemara Mountains lyin' behind 'm like ghosts of mountains.

"Six years I've lived here a bricklayer, out of work often, shamed o' me own name, afeard o' me own shadow, wid niver a friend in the world but the dhrink—the cursed dhrink!

"Ah, no! Why should I curse 't? when I was a sthrong man I cursed 't—when I wasn't hungerin' for 't, dyin' for th' smell of 't, the warmth of 't, th' strength of 't, the tingle of 't on me tongue. 'T has been the ruin o' me, 't has brought me here, 'tis the death o' me now. But 't has been me friend, light in the darkness to me. What else could cheer ye when the pitaties are black in the sodden acre, an' the rain splashes for days long wid niver a hush, an' the wind from the say rattles your door, howlin' like a damned soul, chokin' the shmoke down the chimney-hole till your cabin is blind wid 't, dhrivin' the rain through the chinks o' the door, an' the crannies o' the wall where the plasther 's fallen, an' the leaks o' the roof where the the thatch 's rotten, till the floor turns to mud unther your feet, an' ye sit wid niver a light to burn, niver a morsel t' ate, alone in your misery? What else could brighten ye, be food an' warmth till ye forget the throuble behind an' afore ye, an' see nothin' but hope, an' wouldn't change your cabin for Castle Desmond itself?"

By this time his voice was faint; when his face was towards the wall I could scarcely hear him.

The room was getting darker; the twilight showed only his big square hands, they looked white in the dusk. After a long pause he went on again, talking of Moher and Castle Desmond, of Father Flannery and "Miss Aileen," names familiar to me. He kept speaking of his moonlighting deeds and rather with pride than with repentance; he seemed kindly-natured enough, a man loving his country and his own folk, and yet could see nothing shameful in murder or in maiming cattle.

But the air of the room was sickening, and I was tired of balancing myself on that rickety chair, so I got up to leave him.

Was there anything I could do for him or get for him?

"No, thankin' ye kindly, sir. 'Tis all the same now. All I want is fresh air, an' that ye can't give me in this hell. May ye niver know what 't is to be stharvin' for a glimpse o' clane sky, sthranglin' for fresh air."

Out of doors it was nearly dark. Over the opposite house a flushed moon was rising " in a mist wid a cryin' face on her."

Because it was Saturday the slum was noisy and thronged. Queen's Road was lined by costers' barrows with flaring lights. Swarms of people were about; bareheaded women were chattering and chaffering.

There was a shrill discord of voices and the street reeked with bad smells.

Next morning I again went that way. The small girl told me that McCaura, after I had gone, lay quiet for a time, and that then he said he was going to the top of the slum to get fresh air, and—though he could hardly stand—managed slowly to dress himself, and went up towards Queen's Road tottering and staggering. Soon after—she told me—two neighbours helped him home between them; they had found him fainting at the mouth of the slum, and as they had been drinking they took it for granted that he was drunk, and bringing him they howled a song—

> " As we wos goin' down Bethnal Green
> Jones and I with a gal between."

When they got him down to his cellar he fell heavily across the bundle of rags, and she found him so in the morning; he had left Paradise Walk in search of another Paradise.

.

THE DARK MAN

LONG ago, the Fairies often stole children; they chose the prettiest, and carried them to Fairyland—the Kingdom of Tyrnanoge—leaving hideous Changelings instead. In those days no man had call to be ashamed of his offspring, since if a baby was deformed or idiotic it was known to be a Changeling.

It is sixty years now since old Mike Lonergan, who lived in a hovel in Moher Village, was robbed of his child. It was his wife first found out the theft, for she had seen her unborn son in a dream, and he was beautiful; so when she saw the sickly and ugly baby, she knew that he was not hers, and that the Fairies had stolen the child of her dream. Many advised her to roast the Changeling on the turf-fire, but the White Witch of Moher said it would be safer to leave him alone. So the child Andy grew up as a stranger in his father's hovel and had a dreary time of it, he got little food and no kindness. The Lonergans gave him neither offence nor welcome, hoping that he might see fit to go home to Fairyland, and yet bear them no grudge. He grew up an odd wizened little wretch, and every one shunned him. The children loathed him because they were afraid of him, so they hooted him from a distance or stoned him from behind walls.

Indeed, at this time his only ally was the pig that lived in one corner of the hovel. The pig was a friendly animal, his front half was a dull white and the other half black, and this gave him a homely look as if he was sitting in his shirt-sleeves. Andy would shrink into a corner, and sit cuddled there with one arm round the pig's neck. Old Mike Lonergan took to drink, and spent every evening at the shebeen, small blame to him! for how could a man be expected to stay at home with a Changeling sitting in a corner and staring at him? He complained that even at night, when the pig was snoring and the smoky cabin was only lit by the waning turf-fire, he could still see the child's glowering eyes; for Andy was wakeful and used to wriggle off the shelf that had been fitted as a bed for him (since no one could sleep with a Changeling) and snuggle against the warm flank of his comrade.

When the pig was driven to the Fair at Ennistimon, Andy was left friendless (for the new pig was lean and morose) and then in all winds and weather

he was to be found on the Cliffs of Moher. Sometimes he stopped out all night, till hunger would
bring him back when the Lonergans were rejoicing at
his disappearance. He knew every inch of the Cliffs,
and spent half his time lying on the edge of the
grey precipice, looking down at the sea, six hundred
feet below, or watching the clouds of sea-birds. He
found new paths down the cliff-side and clambered
like a goat. He knew where the gulls nested, but
never robbed them, and the caves where the seals
lived, and the seals shouldered their way through
the water close by him, looking at him with soft
eyes.

When he was about fourteen, the Famine Year
came; fever and "The Hunger" swept Clare. The
fever took Lonergan and his wife, and they were
buried in the dead-pit at Liscannor; it left Andy,
but it left him blind. Then the neighbours began to
have their doubts whether he was a Changeling after
all; for the Fairies are faithful, and who ever heard
of a Changeling being left blind and penniless?
If he was only mortal he had been cruelly treated;
so to make amends they gave him the fiddle that
had belonged to the "Dark" Man—that is the blind
man—of St. Bridget's Well, who had lately starved.
There was still a feeling that he was unfit for a Holy
Well; so he took up a post at the Liscannor Cross-

roads, and there levied a toll on passers with the professional heart-broken cry :

"Remember the Dark Man! For God's sake, remember the Dark Man!"

For nearly twenty years Andy haunted the Cross-roads; he came to be honoured as one of the institutions of Moher, though the folk considered there was much that was uncanny about him, he was so silent and he hated the smell of whisky. He went to his post every morning with such steadiness that Mary Shaughnessy used to say that the noise of his stick on the road was better than a clock to her. And every one he met gave him a kind and respectful greeting. He spent his evenings alone, lying curled up on his hearth like a dog, staring at the spluttering turf with blind eyes.

This was his best time, yet even then he had a lonesome and hard life. Often in winter he came very near starving, for the passers by the Cross-roads had then seldom a halfpenny to spare. He never begged from any one except at the Cross-roads, and his dog Bonaparte would not have taken alms in his tin can anywhere else. But Larry Ronan the blacksmith watched tenderly over him. Larry—who is childless and has a stern wife—needs some to protect, and has made himself guardian of every cripple and witless in County Clare; neglected children look to him for sugarsticks and pelted dogs fly to him for refuge. When the snow sheeted the moors and had like to have soaked Andy's roof, it was Larry climbed up and cleared the thatch. When the window was broken, it was Larry mended it with an old pair of trousers; "for sure," said he, "a dark man can see as far through them as through glass." When the blind man was starving silently, it was Larry stocked the cabin with meal and potatoes that himself could ill spare, but he told me he did it " unbeknownst, for Dark Andy was terrible proud."

Now those were the times when Cornelius Desmond ruled Moher in the old kindly haphazard way, never troubling penniless tenants. But "Corney" died and the daisies grew over him, and then Madden the Agent speedily evicted Dark Andy. He did not seem to know his misfortune; he spent the day of the eviction, as usual, at the Cross-roads, and came back at night to a ruin. Larry Ronan saw that he took the change as a matter of course, and that after groping in the four corners of the cabin he sat on the window-ledge as if unaware that nothing was left of his home but the walls.

Next day it was rumoured that Bridget McCaura, of Moher Farm, had sheltered Dark Andy. Bridget was a warm woman, a "woman of three cows," a masterful old maid, who in her time had refused many a pretty fellow, perhaps because she suspected them of hankering after her live stock, her poultry, and her sixty acres of rocks. Then Father Peter Flannery rode over to see her. Bridget was called out of her house to speak to him; he was afraid to dismount. She stood in the narrow gateway in front of her farm, with her arms akimbo, ready to defend her home against all comers. Peter's heart trembled; he has a great dread of angry women.

"Is it thrue?" he asked—and was so frightened that he looked even sterner than usual—"is it thrue what I'm afther hearing, Bridget McCaura, that ye've taken the Dark Man, Lonergan, to live with ye—to live in the Farm?"

"Is it thrue? 'Tis so," said Bridget.

"But ye're not going to keep him, are ye now?"

"Keep him? I am that," said Bridget.

Peter screwed up his courage and told her warily, that though it was well-meant of her, and "'Tis you have the kind warm heart, Bridget me dear," still, that propriety forbade it.

He was afraid to look at her as he spoke. Bridget was purple.

"What! a misfortnit ould omadhaun the likes of that?" she cried.

"I know, I know," said Peter (this is a pet phrase

"FATHER PETER SCREWED UP HIS COURAGE"

of his and usually means that he does not know)
'I know, I know, but 'tis because ye're a lone

woman, tell me now are ye listening to me? If ye'd been married now, 'twould have been another thing."

"Married!" cried Bridget with infinite scorn— "Married! If that's all, I'll marry the craythur to-morrow!"

And so Dark Andy was married to the richest woman in Moher. He seemed indifferent; as for Bridget, she had made up her mind to shelter him, and there was an end of it, she took pleasure in astounding her neighbours.

There was never such excitement in Clare as when those banns were read. Every one saw that poor Bridget McCaura—"dacint woman"—had been bewitched. All the old stories about Dark Andy came to life, there was no room for doubt now, and the bravest unbelievers trembled before him. There was many a woman would never hear his name without crossing herself, and he got the credit of every misfortune between Kilkee and Kinvarra, though some doubted whether a blind man could have the Evil Eye. It was felt that he should be asked to give up his post by the Cross-roads, since it was inconvenient for the neighbours to have to climb two stone walls to avoid passing him. However, no one could be found to suggest this to him, so he still sat there daily, for he liked to feel that he was earning his own livelihood. His dog still took coppers because nobody dared withhold them. But I have been told that he made no use of this grudged tribute, and buried the coins under the trees.

One rough afternoon during my first visit to Clare I was caught in a storm of rain, and took refuge at the Liscannor Cross-roads under a thick clump of trees that are stunted and bent eastward by cowering from the sea-wind. As I reached them I heard a shrill cry, "Remember the Dark Man!" Then I saw the blind beggarman sitting huddled in a ragged great-coat so much too big for him that till he stood up I did not see how tiny he was. He had a doleful peaked face, set in a shock of grey hair. By him sat a little brown dog—the queerest of mongrels—with a tin can tied round his neck.

Andy was friendly that day, and talked eagerly in a shrill stammering voice. I found later that he was wretched in still weather, and loved the malicious rush of the rain; he was happiest when the wind rattled in his ears and the rain whipped his face. "Call that rain?" he said, "sure th' air is flooded, an' ye might as well swim as walk."

Many times after that I went out of my way on my long solitary walks to pass the Cross-roads, but

"ON THE CLIFFS OF MOHER"

as often as not he was glum and silent, and then Bonaparte, sharing his mood, would growl like a small thunderstorm. The seat was well chosen, for the cowering trees are like a shed over it, and there is a pleasant landscape in front (though that mattered little to Andy), a landscape of dim green moors— with brown stains on them where sedge grows and black shadows where bushes huddle in clefts— chequered by a grey net of low walls, dotted with the white gables of cabins, and framed by a wavering line of hills.

Sometimes I found him playing his fiddle to keep himself company, but he stopped when he heard me, and, to tell the truth, I was glad of it, for his playing was uncanny. Sometimes I met him shambling along the brink of the Cliffs—a grotesque little figure, with his old shapeless hat, his huge coat flapping behind him, and the mighty blackthorn he carried—he knew the ground so well he walked as if he could see (indeed, he saw more than I could, for while to me the breakers were only streaks of light, he spoke as if he was close to them on the wet weedy rocks), or I came on him lying by the edge, listening to the squeaks of the gulls and to the grumbling of the breakers, that monotonous chorus.

No one knew more of folk-lore—I think he half believed that he was a Changeling, and found comfort in the thought of that former life when he was one of the merry "Little Good People"—and sure old Mike Lonergan and his wife ought to have known best. He knew the ways of every ghost in the county, and it was well known that he was on speaking terms with the Headless Man who haunted Liscannor. Of course he knew all about Fairies. When the fallen leaves scurried past his feet he knew that the "Little Good People" were playing football; when the wind whispered in the leaves overhead, he heard them chatting ; and when it whined in the creaking bare branches, heard the poor little folk crying with cold and bewailing the days when they found shelter by snug firesides and sat there unseen but not unwelcome. Once, before the world grew hard, they gathered in the cabins, and the roughest fare grew pleasanter, the saddest hearts lighter, from their good wishes ; but no one cares for them now and they cannot rest in unfriendly houses.

I only once saw him at Moher Farm; it was a fine house with a real chimney—instead of a hole in the thatch to let the smoke out—and boasted three rooms, the two smaller had been made by partitioning off the gable-ends. He was sitting by the open hearth in the big room; it was cosy and one side was fashionably covered with unfashionable crockery and the others were made beautiful by life-like portraits of leading politicians. In one corner a hen was chuckling hysterically, and near her a pig—stretched at full length—blinked at her with gloomy eyes, as if he suspected that it was at him she was laughing. Though there was a pig-stye and a fowl-house in the yard, they preferred human society. Bridget was broad and determined. She seemed to treat Andy with a stern kindness, but that was one of his black days and it was hard to get a word out of him.

I remember thinking that—like the Fairies—he could only be happy when he was alone or with those who were fond of him, that he would gladly have given the comfort of the Farm for the bare walls and the scanty and crazy furniture of his cabin, and that he could not look back without repining on the time when he was penniless and had no friends. Now he shunned the Village, for if he passed through it the chattering groups and the gossips shouting conversations across the street from their doorways grew suddenly silent, and the children ran frightened into their homes. He had no friend left but Larry Ronan, who is a man of so big and warm a heart that he loves everybody except his own wife. But Larry is fond of so many that few value his affection.

Sometimes I found Larry sitting with Andy under

the trees. The grave courtesy of the couple was wonderful; it was "Misther Lonergan, sir," and "Misther Ronan" between them. For that matter one often sees a fine courtesy among the older peasants in Ireland. Last summer as I was driving along the Lisdoonvarna Road, a scarecrow of an old woman, squatting on a heap of stones by the road-side, hailed my ragged driver. "Askin' your pardon, sir," she said, "but did ye happen to meet a loaf on the road? I'm thinkin' I dropt one as I was comin'." "A loaf, is it, ma'am?" he answered, most respect-fully, taking off his hat with a flourish, "a loaf, is it, ma'am? I'm sorry I did not then." "Who was she?" I asked him. "Sure, an' I don't know then," he said, "'tis some poor ould body that's lost her loaf and will be goin' to bed hungry to-night."

As Andy grew older, he talked more of the Fairies— and sometimes with a childishness that had been mis-sing from his desolate childhood—grew more moody and restless, could not sit quiet while the wind was up, and spent night after night out of doors. My friend Father Peter Flannery, who, next to Larry Ronan, is my chief authority for this history, told me that often, riding on his sick calls by night in stormy weather, he met Andy staggering along the rough roads.

At last, one November Eve—the night when the Fairies have power, and the dead wake and dance reels with them—the blind beggarman started out from the Farm. An Atlantic gale was shattering seas against the Cliffs; the air was salt with foam, and throbbed with the pulse of the breakers. Bridget tried in vain to stop him; he said the "Little Good People" were calling him. She watched him disappear into the darkness; the whimpering of his fiddle died into the shrieks of the wind. "'Tis a quare divil, he is," she said, "God help him!"

Once in the night she thought she heard a snatch of the "Fairies' Reel"; but Andy never came back. Next morning they found Bonaparte whining on the edge of the Cliffs; there was no sign of his master. He must have gone over the Cliffs in the darkness, but the waves gave no token.

Some folk in Moher believe that the Fairies took back their child, and that the old blind fiddler lives now in the Kingdom of Tyrnanoge, and makes music for their dances in that enchanted country where the old grow young and the blind see. Some say that he still haunts the Cross-roads, and recently Larry Ronan, coming back late from the Ennistimon Fair, saw a black shadowy figure under the black trees, and heard a heart-broken voice cry, "Remember

K

the Dark Man!" Larry's surprise accounted for his being found next morning asleep in the ditch. But it is agreed in Moher that Andy left life on November Eve, whether he became the playfellow of the Fairies or the plaything of the waves.

AILEEN DESMOND

THE terrace in front of Castle Desmond was a favourite walk of mine when I was first staying with Shane; his sister Aileen was in Dublin, so we had the house to ourselves. Shane spent half his time with his dogs and horses, I spent half my time strolling up and down the terrace reading, but for the rest of the day we were together. We have been staunch friends ever since the year when we—who were then small boys with wild brogues—were sent to an English school. There is no maudlin stuff in our friendship; but for all that, no man could want a more loyal friend. And in those days I was in love with Aileen Desmond.

Well, one sunny afternoon I was sitting on the wall of the terrace in great content. Though I had a book open I was not reading but was thinking of Aileen. I used then to keep thinking of her at irrational times. When I was reluctantly discussing business or politics, suddenly the thought of her

came ; often what I was reading turned to nonsense
and I found I had been hearing her voice ; and if I
woke in the dead of night, her name chimed in
my ears. I was sure then no one in the world's
history had ever the like experience, but am not
so sure of it now. That afternoon I was retracing
my last walk with her along the footpath skirting
the brink of the Cliffs of Moher, a delightful walk,
and who could have wished for a more delightful
companion ? Aileen had in her ways so brave a
simplicity and such a kindly comradeship that even
the youngest men forgot when with her that she was
a girl and spoke to her as if they thought her
intelligence equal to their own. She was by no
means bookish—" it was not given Pompilia to
know much "—but I think I liked her the more.

On our left ran the precipice, with the fringe of
breakers at the foot of it, and every now and then
sudden clouds of sea-gulls shot out from below like
the smoke of guns ; while on our right stretched the
moors of Clare with their bogs and brown hills in a
monotonous succession. We passed Dark Andy, and
I said that he was a type of Ireland fallen now on
evil days, a Changeling in prosy times finding some
comfort in remembering or imagining past happiness.
For I was a prig then, and wished Aileen to see that
I had a poetic soul. I remember her demure serious-

ness when I soared into high-flown phrases. I felt sure that she was awed by my intellect, but I have an idea now that she was laughing in her heart. In those times she could never be grave, and there was always a laugh hiding in her eyes. Nowadays she looks grave enough often. And even as I said it the thought struck me that herself was a type of that other Ireland of the poets, the girl " Dark Rosaleen," always young-hearted and hopeful in spite of Fate. But nothing could have made me put that into words, for though my heart grovelled before her I dared not have come near flattering her. Indeed, I was often abrupt and almost rude to her, just because I was longing to kneel down and worship her. But young Sir Turlogh Davern used to flatter her from morning till night. Often, too, I was silent and if I could get her talking—no matter of what slight foolish things —would listen to her by the hour ; no doubt she then found me a dull and tongue-tied companion, yet sure it was right that I should rather have been hearing her voice than my own.

I could never abide Davern ; he had a conquering way and seemed to think Aileen should have gloried in his admiration. It did not dawn on him that he was a commonplace youth, and that there were thousands like him. I used then to pride myself on being original and singular : and now I think that if

I was so, it was a good thing for the world; and
I know that if my originality had interested Aileen
—as I used to hope—her interest would have been
such as she might have taken in a singular beetle.
She loved common paths and every-day folk. Then,
I loathed all my rivals, and this meant much, for I
counted on the rivalry of every unmarried man who
knew her: now I like all who once cared for her—
except of course Davern—and it was wonderful how
McCaura changed to me when I found that he had
been wounded by her young eyes. When I compared myself with Aileen, I was chilled by my un-
worthiness; but when I thought of other men with
her, I felt they were still less worthy. I had a keen
contempt for myself, but a keener for my rivals,
and chiefly I hated Davern.

At this point of my meditations I saw Shane
coming down the steps to the terrace. He had a
letter in his hand and a big retriever was lumbering
after him. I saw at a glance that he was in one of
his rages, though he had been most cheerful at
lunch; he gave me an angry aggrieved look, but
that was no wonder for when he is in a fury he
burns against all the world impartially. At first I
thought he would have passed without speaking, but
he turned and said in his curtest way:

"Just had a letter from Aileen."

Then at once I grew cold. Any bad news of her was bad for me too. My heart sickened; I had a sense of disaster.

"She's not coming back," he said; "she's engaged to Turlogh Davern."

"Indeed?" I said, "always thought she'd marry him." (This was a lie, but I scarcely knew what I was saying.) "Congratulate her from me, won't you?"

He scowled at me as if I had insulted him, then he strode off to the garden and as he went I saw him kick the retriever. Now Shane must be savage indeed before he kicks his dogs.

I watched him going. I hardly seemed to realise what he had said. Aileen engaged? it seemed incredible; and yet surely I had known it for a long time. Then I re-opened my book and bent over it intently. I felt as if every window in the Castle had a face staring at me to see how I took the news. I would show them I was too much of a man to care for the whims of a girl. (Only four old servants were in the house, and they could have known nothing of the engagement.) I used to love the reverend face of the Castle, but now it had a new look and stared at me with glassy eyes, the very ivy clambering up and clinging to the gap-toothed battlements had innumerable pricked ears. At first, I know, I was resentful; I felt my cheeks burning. Then my mood altered to a bitter humility; that I should have been hopeful of winning Aileen seemed no less than a sacrilege. Then the thought of Davern stung me to pride; had she have chosen any other man in the world I could have borne it. I felt I had nothing more to live for, my hopes and dreams were dead; and I was sure it was all Shane's fault, he must have been against me just because he knew I was poor. Now that I came to think of it, he had never given me a word of encouragement though he must have known I worshipped the girl. Why, any man with eyes in his head would have seen it. I used to try and look at her with studied indifference, but never could. When I looked at her it was with worshipping eyes, my soul was in my face. And I took bitter shame that I had been so unmanly as to set all my heart on a girl. In those days I set great store on my manliness; you know I was a boy then.

I have no notion how long it was before I found that my cigarette had gone out, and that I was holding the book up-side-down. It had grown late, and I remember noticing that the still sea looked white. I felt that I had sufficiently asserted my dignity and callousness, so I threw the cigarette away, shut the book, and went into the house with a cheerful swagger—

still braving those staring windows—but I had a lump in my throat.

Looking back now, I find that I never bore Aileen a grudge though I was sore with Shane and fierce against Davern. She always met me with the same friendliness ; probably she never dreamt of my court-ship. Once I remember seeing her going about silent and with a white face because that outrageous Davern had delayed writing to her, then how gladly I would have thrown him over the Cliffs of Moher! And I know now that I would have suited her ill. She is the loving mother of a small Davern, she is very tranquil and is sweet to every one whether she likes them or loathes them, has rid herself of her brogue and caught the delightful " English " accent that is the chief charm of Dublin society : but when we were young at Castle Desmond she was not ashamed of her brogue or of her likes and dislikes, and I who have lived among books till the dust of them has made my eyes dim and my heart dry would be a queer mate for her.

I know that in this—my one love affair—I cut a sorry figure. What sight could be more ludicrous than the ugly and despairing lover of a pretty girl, a lover too cowardly to try his luck and too vain to risk a refusal ? It was prophetic of my life, a pro-

phecy of failure. It is not strange that I, beginning
with such faintheartedness, should drowse through the
ineffectual life of a bookworm in these dusty chambers,
with no keener anxiety than the daily dread that
some stranger may have taken my favourite seat in
the Museum Library, with no wilder pleasure than
the round of the secondhand bookstalls between the
Museum and the Temple.

Sometimes in my younger days I blasphemed
against Aileen, saying to myself that she was after all
a shallow and commonplace girl, and condemning the
more bitterly the folly of my craze for her. But now
I am ready to own that she was ordinary, and am
not prig enough to find that a fault. Indeed I think
it was the simple health of her nature that conquered
me. Nor was there anything rare about the type of
her looks. One rainy night I remember—in the time
when I was maddest about her—as I was hurrying
along the Strand, a glimpse of a wax figure in a
barber's window brought my heart to my mouth, it
was so like Aileen as I had last seen her at The
O'Mulligan's dance.

Well, I saw nothing of Shane till dinner-time,
and then we spoke little and discussed the weather
and politics, though we both hated both subjects.
Afterwards we sat by the fireside and smoked with

glum faces, each of us angry with the other for being angry with him.

We stared at the blazing logs, each busy with his own thoughts. For the life of me, I could not help thinking of Aileen; her chair was in the dark corner, every now and then the light caught it and then the carved lions' heads on the handles grinned at me. She was in that dull house in Merrion Square, it was not dull to her now if Davern was with her; perhaps he had his arm round her waist. To tell the truth I had a very sore heart. I am not certain that to think Shane had been against me was not the bitterest. Aileen could do no wrong, I never had any chance with her, besides she was only a girl : but Shane was my friend, ever since we were brats in knicker-bockers we had been comrades ; I used to think that whatever might happen—through good report or ill report—I could count on Shane.

I had no thought of reproaching him ; I was too sore and too proud. As for Shane, I knew he would see me to the Devil before he would excuse himself for anything. There was no sound in the room except the rustling and lapping of flames and the crackling of the logs. Suddenly, because I had fully made up my mind to hold my tongue, I spoke out :

" I thought you would have stood by me, Shane."

He knew what I meant, he must have been think-

ing of the same things.   He did not look at me, and
spoke with wonderful meekness:

"To tell the truth," he said, " I'm as sorry about
it as you are" (this was absurd) " and she likes you
greatly, of course, but you know you never had the
ghost of a chance.   Why, he had the pull of you
every way.   He's a hunting man and a dancing man
and all the rest of it, while you spend half your time
with your head in a book ; you're a silent beggar, he
talks like a mill-stream ; he has lashings of money,
and you haven't a penny to bless yourself with ; "
(this I thought needlessly frank) " and what's more
he isn't half bad looking."   I grinned ruefully.

" I don't care if the fool is a millionaire Apollo,"
I said, " you should have backed me all the same."

"And didn't I back you all along, man ?" asked
Shane, angrily jumping up from his chair.   " Confound you, what an ass you are."   He was exceedingly red in the face ; he took my hand and crushed
it.

" Why, damn it, old man, don't ye know I'd rather
you were married to Aileen than a dozen Daverns ! "

A PRODIGAL

I

LATE one night I was sitting by the fireside in the
dining-room at Castle Desmond. The sea-wind was
crooning round the old house and whining in the
wide chimney. Though the others had gone to bed,
I could not tear myself away from the fire; it was
burning low and casting a fickle twilight into the
long room behind me. That is the light the ghosts
love now; you might walk the world by moonlight
and never meet one of them, but if you would see
them it must be by their old hearths, revisiting the
glimpses of the firelight. I could see one then, but
there was nothing uncanny about it, it had winning
eyes and a wheedling brogue for it was Aileen
Desmond's ghost and Aileen had only left the
room a few minutes before. As she went she put
out the lamp, saying laughingly that it would be
a pity to let such prosy light disturb my mournful

meditations. I could still see her quite plainly in her big chair—when the light flickered on it and on the yawning lions' heads carved on its handles—and I could hear her soft voice and her softer laugh quite plainly; but there was a sameness about her remarks, for they were the echoes of what she had been saying that evening.

Then I said to myself, " If all the ghosts of all the Desmonds haunted this room like Aileen we'd be a merry meeting." And I thought of some of the queer doings in this dining-room in the rackety days when those logs had young life in them and many a coach and six swept noisily up the long avenue through the park and periwigged bucks went courting under the trees.

I began to feel creepy, for the firelight was jerking, and I knew it was peopling the room with shadows, and the old furniture had an unpleasant way of creaking of its own accord as if some one was moving it. The fire was smouldering, and the darkness behind was closing round me: when suddenly the wreck of piled logs fell in, a new tongue of flame flared up the chimney, and a new light was flung out into the black room.

Startled by the change I turned and looked round. Then I saw it was indeed a change, for the long table was lit up by a double row of wax candles that brightened a white tablecloth with much silver and tall glass ware on it, and the relics of a profuse feast, many glasses were broken, and the cloth was stained by spilt wine. The chairs near me were empty, but towards the far end of the table a number of men — some twenty I thought — sat drinking. They wore the dress of two hundred years ago—full blown periwigs and gorgeous coats and lace ruffles—and I at once knew many of them from the old portraits.

That big red man in rich purple at the head of the table was Sir Hercules Desmond; the elderly soldier on his right was Lord Theobald Butler; that old man on the left fast asleep, sunk back in his chair, looking like a corpse with his jaw dropped and his yellow chalk-stoned hand spread flat on the table, was Major Theophilus Blake, who had once been a famous duellist.

Some of the men were mighty young, and most seemed to have done their share of the drinking; one chair was lying on the ground—I supposed its owner was under the table—one man was asleep with his bare head laid on his folded arms among his broken glasses, his wig had fallen off, or perhaps somebody had snatched it, his shaven skull was a queer contrast to his flushed face and red neck. The calmest was my Lord Kilkee, a cold-blooded languid youth with a narrow proud face; as he leant his head on the back of his chair the apple of his throat was shown oddly against his neighbour's periwig.

Most of the company were looking towards Sir Hercules, he had his head thrown back and his mouth wide open. I knew he was singing by the throbbing of his red throat and the wagging of his chin; I saw that it was a rollicking song by his way, and that it was unseemly by the conscious look of some of the younger men.

Now next Theophilus Blake I saw a fellow— a mere boy—with a face long familiar, a handsome devil-may-care face, the living image of one of my friends. He was haggard and flushed, his wig was tilted awry and some of the white powder from it had fallen on his scarlet coat. Once he laughed at a verse of the song; then he sat looking down the table towards me with a strange look and wide open eyes.

At that moment Sir Hercules stopped singing, and refilled his glass with a shaky hand—he spilt half the claret—then he lolled back as if he felt he had done his duty, and the others turned to one another laughing and talking. Suddenly every man started as if at a shot. Old Theophilus Blake woke with a jump as if it was the Day of Judgment; even the bareheaded man looked up slowly.

"HE SEEMED TURNED TO A RANTING PREACHER"

L

The boy had sprung to his feet, seemed to be calling out aloud, seemed turned to a Ranting Preacher; he had a gesture of passionate warning and pleading with his hands flung out high with the palms towards me, and the look of a prophet calling on the people of a doomed city to mend their ways while there was yet time.

The company stared as if they could not believe their eyes; one man grabbed angrily at his left side to draw his rapier, forgetting that no one was armed; old Theophilus Blake shrank away nervously; the bare-headed man dropped his heavy head on his arms and slept; my Lord Kilkee leant forward and smiled blandly.

Sir Hercules wore a look of ludicrous astonishment and his face was nearly as purple as his coat; then he seemed to understand, his mouth widened into a jolly smile; he stretched across Theophilus and laid his big left hand on the boy's scarlet sleeve, his smile and his gesture spoke so plainly that I seemed to hear "Sit down now, boy, don't ye know you're drunk?" Lord Theobald flung himself back in his chair with his hands on his sides, and with such a laugh that the candle in front of him nearly went out. My Lord Kilkee said something—with that pale smile of his and with raised eyebrows—as he lolled back. I knew too what he was saying.

" For my part I think he's mad," said my Lord Kilkee.

At that moment the blaze suddenly died, and the long room became pitch dark. I turned back to the hearth ; the charred ruin of the great log lay flat and little upstart flames were dancing on it not knowing that their life would end with its death. And I knew that this dream of mine was a memory of a strange scene in London.

II

I HAD a friend once who was a countryman of mine and came from Monkstown in County Cork. He was in London for a fortnight, five years ago now, on his way to Australia in search of a fortune. I saw little of him, he was much the younger ; our friendship rose from a meeting at Castle Desmond, and I had grown to be a bookworm. Some nights he came round to my chambers ; I could hear him a long way off, startling the silent courts of the Temple with his Irish songs for he spent half his time singing. Sometimes I met him in the Strand walking with an air as if he owned London, beaming at everybody, swinging his stick and humming as if he was on a country road.

One night I had settled down to a quiet evening,

sunk in my big armchair with half a dozen books
piled within easy reach. I remember I was reading
Burton, and had got to the passage, " Hoffemannus
relates out of Plato how that Empedocles "—when I
heard him coming up the dark stairs three steps at
a time; he was always at full speed except when he
was plunged in despair and that was seldom enough.
He stumbled over a bucket on the landing—usually,
one is left there to trip strangers—then he thundered
on my outer door with his walking stick.

" Come out of that now. You're in. Don't deny
it man," he shouted.

I let him in, telling him mildly that there was no
need to wake the dead.

" And there's many a dead man in the Old Country
that has more life in him than you," he said. " Don't
they dance reels on November Eve with the Fairies?
and when did you ever dance a reel?"

The boy was in wild spirits, and wore evening
dress, with a gardenia in his buttonhole; he looked
absurdly handsome.

" Hang it! old man," he said, sitting on my table
and throwing his stick on my desk; " Hang it! what
an old dormouse you are. To see you poking over
your everlasting books, with nothing but books round
you, one would think you were as old as the hills.
What's that you're reading? 'The Anatomy of

Melancholy,' as I'm a living sinner! Put away that musty stuff and come out with Foster and me."

"Nonsense," I said, "I've settled down to an evening's peace."

"And what d'ye want with peace at your age, man? Is it an Irishman y'are at all? Why, it's fighting y' ought to be looking for."

But I was too lazy; it would have taken a great deal to make me go into evening dress at that hour, so the end of it was that he and Foster went off.   As they went up the court I could hear him singing— like a bird, as he would have said—

> " Oh, rise up, William Reilly,
>   And come along with me ! "

till his voice died in the distance.

And I went on cheerfully reading Burton where I had left off, "how that Empedocles the philosopher was present at the cutting up of one that died for love: his heart was combust, his liver smoakie, his lungs dried up, insomuch that he verily believed his soul was either sod or rosted through the vehemency of love's fire."

Afterwards, Foster told me a singular story. It seems they walked down the Strand arm-in-arm; though the hour was late the street was fuller and noisier than in the daytime, and my friend found it more interesting than any theatre. As he was a stranger, Foster took him to see the Aspasian Club. They had supper in the crowded supper-room, and my friend was in such spirits that many at the other tables looked round at him, thinking he had taken more wine than was good for him, though he had drunk little. Then they went into the long smoking-room. It was full of men and women in evening dress, but he wondered at their quietness; this was by no means his young idea of revelry.

On one side of the smoking-room there is a balcony, and you can look down from it on the ball-room on the floor below. He stood there some time; a band was playing, and many couples were waltzing; it was a pretty sight.

"They're pretty girls, too," he said to Foster, "it's a pity they're no better than they ought to be—though you might say that of most of us." He seemed to have suddenly grown moody and spoke little.

Foster left him and joined a group of his acquaintance; there was young Lord Kilkee—a pale bland youth with a narrow conceited face—there was Lilian de Vere, who looks like an innocent Dresden china shepherdess, and General Vereker, that old tottering reprobate, and perky little Phœbe Woodbine—the

Gaiety dancer—who looks as if she is half an angel and half a pug, and Caterina Moroni who was once Kitty Moroney of Skibbereen.

Suddenly Foster heard some one speaking in a very loud voice. Every one started and looked towards the balcony.

"And there," said Foster to me, "there was that boy preaching, upon my soul! preaching to the people in the ball-room! Goodness knows what he was saying; I couldn't believe my ears. He looked as if he was turned to a cracked Salvationist; he had his hands flung out high, and he was calling on the people to leave their sins, to turn to God while there was yet time, for the night was coming, the Night of God.

"For a moment every one was struck breathless. I know Caterina Moroni went white as a sheet. Then there was a shout of laughing all over the room.

"'Turn the fellow out, he's drunk!' cried several.

"'For my part, I think he's mad,' smiled young Lord Kilkee."

A PRODIGAL'S RETURN

AN old ruined Castle stands behind the sleepy village
of Monkstown, by the river Lee. The ruins are
covered with ivy, a wide park lies around them, and
from one corner of the ramparts—where there is a
white rose bush, the last relic of the forsaken garden
—you have a wonderful view of bright wooded country
with the lazy river lounging through it. The village
is clustered round a prim church, and the moated
ramparts rise behind like a cliff.

Kate Langrishe lives in Monkstown—you may meet
her there any day; a quiet girl, with rather a noble
face and with steady eyes—she leads a prosy life with
her old bedridden mother. Some five years ago, Kate
parted from her lover. He was one of those weak
well-meaning fellows it is an affliction to know. You
could not keep from liking him, though you groaned
to think what a fool he could be. Since he was poor,
he went to Australia to make money. The day he
started they strolled up to the Castle together for the

last time. Their way passed the cool church, and
they went in. A big Bible lay on the reading-desk,
and he suggested, half seriously, that they should
each open the book at random to see if the texts they
read first would tell their fortunes. I forgot what
text he read, but Kate opened the book at—

> " When I found him whom my soul loveth,
>   I held him and would not let him go."

Then they went up to their favourite meeting-place
where the white roses grow by the crumbling rampart.
It was a bright April day, the sunshine gave a silver
glimmer to the ivy on the ruins and made the young
leaves on the edges of the trees shine like gold.

He was in one of his absurdly bright moods—was
always going from one extreme to the other, full of
hope or of gloom—spoke of the great things he was
going to do, for he intended to move the world.
Kate listened to him, happy in his hopefulness, though
in her heart she had doubts of his triumph. But what
did that matter if only he did his best ? Well, they
said good-bye there, and she plucked a white rose from
the bush and gave it to him, saying, " Keep the rose
white, dear."

He spent four years in Australia and made no money,
was unchanged, was in scrapes again, he wished he

had never left home. During this time his love for
Kate lived, but it was " the desire of a moth for a

" HE STOPPED UNDER KATE'S WINDOW "

star"—compatible with a weakness for candles—and
the rose rotted in his desk. When he thought of
her now it was with a new reverence, as he grew
older he looked up to her simple goodness.

Often in the dry heat he longed for an hour at home, to breathe the fresh Irish air, to ramble with her through the green lanes, to drive on an outside car along those rough roads winding through the low hills. So, without warning any one—for he had not the heart to write owning his failure—he came back nearly penniless, as a steerage passenger, to see Kate, to begin his life again. The worst of him was that he was always reforming, always beginning again, but never got beyond the beginning; he was as weak as water.

The ship reached Queenstown at night; he crossed the river and tramped across country to Monkstown through familiar fields. It was a damp grey night. In spite of all he was in high spirits, and sang to himself because he was home now and would see Kate; he laughed to think how surprised every one would be.

As he reached the village the watery dawn made the sky a lighter grey; he stopped under Kate's window and his heart fell. There was no light, no sign of life anywhere; this was a wretched home-coming. He walked up the street slowly and silently; the pavement was slippery, the street was clogged with mud, the Castle ramparts hung dimly over him in the twilight; he went up through the ivied gateway. The ruins and trees were black; the wind made a hissing noise in the branches. As he walked through the wet grass his heart was heavy as lead ; the low sky seemed heavy as lead over him. He passed the white rose-bush—there were no buds on it—and standing in the old place leant on the shaky rampart.

Below him he saw the glossy roofs of the village, and closer the green moat choked by nettles and dock-leaves and grass. The wet ivy struck a chill through him ; he was very tired and felt dizzy, the moat seemed drawing him down to it. Then he felt in his breast pocket for the rose—he had brought it to show her he had not forgotten her words—he found it had fallen to pieces, there was nothing of it left but a bit of green stalk and some brown flakes ; he looked at them for a moment, then flung them over the ramparts.

Suddenly he felt grown old and saw his whole life in darkness, it was horrible to look back upon. Now it seemed to him that he must have been mad at times ; he cursed his own weakness, his useless struggles ; if he had made no attempts at better things there would have been hope for him, his struggles to reform damned him. He was coming back to Kate—but what right had he to come ? If he had been strong her love would have been his reward. Surely he had never known her before, she

seemed so infinitely above him; he could think of
her only, the rest of the world was nothing to him,
they two were alone in it.   Now, weaker than ever,
failing hopelessly—what right had he to claim her?
While he lived she would stand by him always, but
for him to take her would be a cad's trick.   Though
he had been a fool, at least he was a gentleman.

Some lines of Swift's ran in his head :

> " For such a fool was never found,
>   Who pulled a palace to the ground,
>   Only to have the ruins made
>   Materials for a house decayed."

He knew he would wreck her life in spite of his
love of her; that was his history, loving the higher
things, following the lower.   This had gone on long
enough; it was time there should be an end of it;
he wished to God that he was dead.   As he leant
forward heavily on the old wall he felt it tottering
and crumbling under him.

Next day they found him lying face downwards in
the moat among the dock-leaves and nettles, under
a new gap where the rampart had fallen.   No one
recognised him, he was buried as a stranger in the
village where he was born.   All the wiseacres in
Monkstown remembered they had always said the

rampart would give way some day or other and kill somebody.

Kate is growing quite an old maid now; no one else remembers her love affair, it was over so long ago, but for her it was not over. She is sure he will come back to her yet; he is rising slowly, having a hard fight of it, but he is upright and honoured. Sometimes she sees him struggling and failing; after all he was only a weak boy, though so well-meaning. No matter how he fails, no matter how he has fallen, he is loyal to her still, he will come back to her some day.

In a dream she saw him coming to her, he was broken and degraded, his clothes were ragged, worn out he fell at her feet; she stretched out her trembling hands to him, took him in her arms, and held him like a mother holding a hurt child, saying:

> " When I found him whom my soul loveth,
> I held him and would not let him go."

THE HEROISM OF LARRY RONAN

My favourite philosopher is Larry Ronan, the black-smith of Moher. A big man and a rollicking is Larry, and no woman in that country-side (except his wife) can look on him with a hard eye. The men like him because he has many faults and is so well aware of them that he is a kind judge of the failings of others. He is the king of the shebeen; often have I found him in it reciting the burning eloquence of the local papers to a breathless circle while his anvil stood silent. His worst fault is his weakness for drink; when sober he is a rational and kindly companion, but drink soon makes him bloodthirsty of speech. When he is very drunk he grows heartbroken; then he has a singular custom: he staggers through the village knocking at every door, "Larry Ronan's dead," he says, "Poor Larry Ronan! God rest his kind soul! They've sent me to bid ye to his wake." When first he said that to Peggy Lonergan she near died of fright; she took him for his own ghost.

But now the women say, " Ah! Misther Ronan, dacint man, won't ye be goin' home now ?" and add, as he staggers down the street, " Ah! the poor man! 'tis Mary Ronan that 'll be rampageous to-night."

But in the eyes of Moher this is a lovable weakness, and his worst fault is his peacefulness—for he is so lazy that he hangs back from fighting —and that is forgiven him because he was a hero once.

Larry and I get on well ; my silence suits him. He is a wonderful talker, full of wise maxims that he never obeys, and yet is a poor story-teller, for he would rather be vaguely and wordily discussing the bettering of the times and the errors of statesmen than be slave to a narrative. In this he reminds me of the Rector who, mid-way in a story, is as like as not to forget all about it, and treat you to a rhapsody on Catullus or on some epigram from the Anthology. But, while the Rector loves to speak of himself, his own history is a subject hateful to Larry, and I could never get him to tell me the story of his heroism till I came on him one afternoon in Liscannor. I had been walking along the brink of the Cliffs of Moher round by the Hag's Head. There was a stiff wind, and the grey sea had white scars on it and showed a jagged rim against the red sunset. As I reached Liscannor I saw Larry sitting on the quay-wall of that

M

starved fishing-village; some chance job had brought him from Moher. He looked glum, and was staring across Liscannor Bay at the white loop where the big seas were rolling in on Lahinch. By the brightening of his face at the sight of me, and the grip of his hand-shake, I knew he was dying for a listener; so I seated myself on the wall by him.

Just then we heard singing, and some dozen young fisher-folk came up the quay arm in arm. They were dirty and dishevelled; one or two, I think, had drunk more than was good for them. As they passed they greeted us with a howl of friendly derision.

"Them craythurs," said Larry, "them craythurs they live yonther, some of them in houses that would sicken a pig; they scarce iver have enough t' ate or a dacint rag to their backs or a dacint shawl to their heads. An' for all that if they've a shillin' they spend it freely, if they've only a penny 'tis as gladly their friend's as their own, an' they're divils to fight. And there they're now, a laffin' an' a singin' and a howlin' just like kings."

Further up the quay they stopped and began dancing hand in hand in a ring, keeping time to their own unmusical singing.

"Just like kings," said Larry, "take them all together I'm blessed if they aren't a good sort.

"What's that ye say, sir? ye thought I didn't hould wid fightin? No more I don't. Ivery man thinks he's a hero till he's thried it; like ivery man thinks he can fool the girls till one of them fools him. But he finds out some day. An' I found out soon enough I didn't like fightin'. For there's small pleasure in thrashin' a man if ye know ye can do it, an' there's less if ye know ye can't; an' if you're not sure aither way, why not lave it so? Not but that I'm quarrelsome when the dhrop's in me. Ah! the dhrink's the great deluther; that's why we like it, for we love bein' deluthed, more by token that's why we love the girls."

"May be," I said, "that's why you're so fond of politics."

"An' that's a thrue word, so it is. We do be sayin' we dhrink to dhrive the cold from our hearts; but sure there's little cold in the heart of an Irishman. An' 'tisn't so much the girls 'mselves—bless 'm!—that we hanker afther; 'tis the wheedlin' 'm an' the palaverin' 'm an' the feedin' 'm wid false music, an' seein' the softness come to their eyes and them blushin' like a fire in the twilight.

"When I was a youngsther there wasn't a colleen in Moher that I hadn't gone courtin', barrin' Mary O'Brien, that lived out yonther by Lahinch where the Cullenagh runs into the say. I was half afeard

of her, more power to me senses for that! she was
a sthrappin' girl, wid bould eyes that could make a
big man feel mighty small and could button your
lips wid a look. 'Twas at Mike Lonergan's weddin'
—him that owned th' ould hooker—that I first took
heart o' grace to thry sootherin' her, bad luck to the
day! Sure she liked the sootherin' so, that afore
night I was mad about her. All the day long I was
hangin' afther her. 'Twas wontherful how fond of
me prayin' I became—she was always at the church
—Father Flannery was proud of me. An' the work
I did at the Farm! if I'd worked so for meself I'd be
a rich man now. Sometimes she was sunshine to
me, and then to see me shwaggerin' about wid me
nose in the air, ye'd 've thought I was Colonel
Herc'les Desmond in disguise; sometimes she wasn't,
an' then ye'd 've thought I was runed an' disgraced.
Well, one morn I was round at the Farm—did I
tell ye she was ould Jim O'Brien's daughter that lived
by Lahinch?—an' a quare little tottherin' omadhaun he was, but a warm man wid a fine farm of 's
own. Th' agent—the Shnipe we call 'm—was always
afther evictin' 'm but he wouldn't go. 'I'll have ye
out by force,' says the Shnipe. 'So ye may, sir,'
says O'Brien, 'but 'twill be feet foremost, an' the
life 'll be out o' me afore I'm out o' me farm.' An'
'twas thrue for him, so it was. He was a desprit

quiet little ould man an' a desprit stubborn—sure Mary takes afther 'm in that annyhow."

"Come now," I said, "I have a deal of respect for Mrs. Ronan."

"Respect is it? an' I have that same. She's a great woman, so she is ; though the more ye see of her, the less ye like her. I'd be terrible fond of her if she was married to some one else. But as I was sayin', 'twas a gran' morn an' I was happy as an Imperor. 'Tis bad to be too happy ; ye may be sure then that throuble's not far off. Did y' iver hear tell of two sthrangers that were climbin' a mountain over behind there in Connemara—one o' the Pins o' Binabola. As they reaches the top o' 't—where there was a wee mist—they races an' the one that was first gives a whoop an' flings 'mself flat to rest, an' th' other side o' the mountain 's no mountain but a precipice, an' the whoop was scarce out of 's mouth afore he was shatthered an' moithered to smithereens. 'Twas so wid ould Jim O'Brien. Mary she sat knittin' in the big chair by the hearth, blushin' like a rose ; badly she was knittin', for I sthood by the chimney lookin' down into th' eyes of her and wheedlin' her. An' ould O'Brien he was potherin' 'bout in the front yard, watchin' us out o' the tail of 's eye ; laffin' he was an' hummin' a quare little tune to 'mself, for he did use to fear Mary 'd be a lone woman all her

days.　An' the fowls they were all clutherin' at once,
an' the pigs—the craythurs—they ran about so as if
they'd 've danced if they could, an' 'twas a gran'
June morn.

"Sudden we hears a shout from the boy that was
always on the hillside watchin' for fear the Shnipe 'd
be afther surprisin' O'Brien, an' we runs to the gate,
an' then toppin' the hill out on the Liscannor Road,
we sees the caps an' the guns o' the consthables an'
the gun-barrels a-shinin'.　Truth to tell, I wished
meself further, but that was past prayin' for.　O'Brien
he runs into the house.　'Quick!' says he, 'bar
the door an' the shutters an' we'll keep 'm out yet!
Run gossoon,' says he to the boy, 'an' call all the
folk to help us!'　'Ah! tis the great luck ye're here
Misther Ronan!' says Mary to me—she that niver
doubted I was brave because I'm big—'tis the way o'
women.　'The divil's own luck!' says I to meself. ·

"There was no help for 't, an' in no time we'd the
door barred an' the table agin't an' the shutther up,
an' we hadn't more than the time afore we heard the
consthables halt in the road.　Ould O'Brien had
hould of 's gun, thrimblin' like he was dyin' o' fright;
he was by me an' Mary beyond, clutchin' 'm, tellin'
'm to be aisy an' lay the gun down.　I could scarce
see her the room was that dark, barrin' the chinks
o' light over the door an' unther it, an' by the edge

of the shutther, an' the roun' o' light on the hearth
unther the chimney. For all the world 'twas like
bein' in a coffin—save us!—an' watchin' the light
through the chink an' knowin' ye were dead an'
could niver get out agin into God's sunlight. An'
I felt cold as a frog, for though I'd face a wipe wid
a shillelagh as soon as annyone, the wrong ind of a
loaded gun is a mighty chill place.

"The consthables they shouted to us to come out o'
that, but we kept sthill tongues; an' we heard the
neighbours callin' an' cursin', but they were small
help barrin' curses an' sthones. 'Tis wastin' time
sthonin' consthables; they're that used to 't that if
ye were to throw mountains at 'm they'd hardly
mind ye.

"Then the Shnipe he comes to the door an' he calls
out, spakin' mighty slow—bad luck to the baste! he
couldn't talk fast if he thried—an' mighty gentle—
like a woman talks to ye till ye've married her.

"'Listen to me now, James O'Brien,' says he,
'don't ye know 'tis no use makin' a hare o' yourself?
'Twill be betther for you now if ye come out o' that,
quick.'

"An' O'Brien, he screeches out, wid a cryin' voice
like an' ould broken woman, 'If I come out o' me
farm, it'll be feet foremost I'll go.'

"'Is that a fact now?' says the Shnipe, ''tis your

own doing, man; mind ye 'tis no fault o' mine '—an'
we hears him tellin' the consthables to smash in the
door wid a pole they'd brought wid 'm. 'Tis a stout
door that'll sthand when half a dozen sthrong men
rushes at it wid a pole.

"'Now!' says the Shnipe, and we hears 'm runnin',
an' then the pole smashes agin the door and shatthers
a hole in 't. The fut o' the pole sthicks into the
room, but the door holds fast. An' they draws the
pole back for another blow; an' the room grows twice
as clare from the light through the hole.

"But ould O'Brien, he gives a cry as if the divil
was in 'm an' he jumps forrard wid his gun, an' he
shoves the table aside, an' he fires through the hole
in the door, an' he falls back from the door; an'
through 't, as the shmoke went, I saw Sergeant
Molloy—the dacintest man in Clare if he hadn't been
a consthable, one that niver refused a dhrink, one
that'd always a word an' a laugh for ye, one that'd
niver see ye if ye were dhrunk—Molloy, he turns
white an' sthaggers agin the man by him. 'God
help me!' says he, whisperin' 'I'm a dead man!'

"O'Brien he turns that sick, ye'd 've thought he
was kilt, not Molloy. He goes an' sits in th' ould
chair by the fire, all in a heap, wid the gun lyin'
across his knees, an' his han's hangin' down, an'
lookin' as if he was a hunthred. Mebbe he saw

"I SURRENTHER, 'TWAS ME THAT DONE IT"

'mself kickin' in th' air wid a rope roun' his neck,
the poor craythur! Then crash comes the pole agin,
an' bruk all the door, an' the polis makes a rush
forrard, one o' them cryin', ' Surrenther!'

"Mary O'Brien she clutches hould o' me elbow,
'Larry!' she cries—an' she that always called me
'Misther Ronan' mighty polite ('tis 'baste' she calls
me now, as often as not)—'Ah! Larry, darlin', says
she, ' for God's sake, save dad!'

" An' I looks at her, an' widout thinkin' a moment
—if I'd thought I'd not 've done 't—I jumps to the
door, an' the light was dazzlin' me, an' there was the
consthables rushin' an' their guns near touchin' me
(glad I'd 've been if they'd kilt me, for hangin's the
black death), ' I surrenther,' I cries, ' I surrenther,
'twas me that done 't.'

" Lord only knows why I did so, I felt as bould as
a bull: mebbe 'twas because th' ould man was such
a poor tiny little craythur, mebbe 'twas because he
was Mary's father, she was a sthar through the mist
then to me, an' thrushes were crows to the voice of
her; manny's the divil of a time she's given me
since, manny's the sore name she's screeched at
me wid that same voice—not but that I've always
desarved 't.

" But ould O'Brien, he makes a rush past me.
' 'Tis a lie,' he cries, ' 'tis a damned lie,' an' fires his

other barrel right at the polis.   That minit they
fired too—they were that close that I thought I was
blind an' deaf for iver ; I thought the flashes lasted
a year—an' O'Brien (God help 'm !) he gives a jump,
dhroppin' 's gun, an' flingin' his han's up in th' air,
an' falls flat on 's back across the threshold, an' the
blood breaks from the mouth of 'm—Ah ! the poor
old man !

" An' that was th' end of 't, an' they dhragged me
off to prison.   An' all Ireland rang wid the fight :
ivery one was sorry for ould O'Brien that died
defendin' his property, an' it's manny were sorry for
John Molloy, that was a kind man an' a fine judge
of potheen, but what else could he expect, an' he a
consthable ?   An' I married Mary, an' all Moher
called me a hero (I don't mane for marryin' Mary ;
that was the brave thing to do, but I didn't know
it), but if I was a hero, 'twas the first time, an' by
the powers I hope it'll be the last."

IN THE BLACK VALLEY

ALL that morning they kept passing under his window in a long procession, with cries of despair and appeal, heart-broken and uncomforted, dragged from the homes they loved to face an unknown fate. From the grey of the dawn there was no pause in their lamentation.

"Confound those pigs!" said Shane Desmond, "sure one might as well be living in Chicago!"

It was the morning of the pig-fair in Killarney, and Shane was sick of life. He had come to Killarney to meet Kitty Geraldine—she was to have stopped there on her way to Queenstown—but there was no sign of her. Yet because he loved her he was more angry with himself than with her; why was he such a fool as to think she could care for him?

During breakfast he kept thinking of all the things she had said and done that had made him hopeful. But now it was wonderful how different a meaning they bore. There was that matter of the

forget-me-nots.   He found them when he was rowing
her on Loch Carra and offered them to her, trem-
blingly and in silence but with a look that spoke
libraries.   She took them as if they were a botanical
curiosity, and later she gave them back to him with
her inscrutable smile.   Then he was wild with delight
for how could she have given him plainer encouragement?   Those weeds became his chief treasure, and
he wore them over his heart, in his waistcoat pocket.
Now he saw that she must have meant to refuse
them; so he decided to destroy the rubbish.

After breakfast he joined the hotel party of sight-
seers, though he was now sure that Killarney was
over-rated.   When he was told that the waggonette
was full and that he must follow on a car, he took
it as an insult.   If he had been asked to drive in the
crowded waggonette the insult would have been as
bitter.   He strode gloomily to the car and mounted
it without even a look at the party in front, for he
was certain they were ludicrous Cockneys exploring
Ireland with mingled contempt and terror, expecting
to be shot by midday Moonlighters, as if any Irishman would waste powder on them.   Kitty had treated
him so badly that he was more than ready to quarrel
with any one or every one else.

It was dull weather, everything aggravated him.
The party had driven some way before he looked with

gloomy scorn at the waggonette in front. Then
suddenly all the world changed, the weather became
delightful, the scenery a dream, the harmless sight-
seers became beautiful and lovable, for there among
them was Kitty Geraldine. She was studying the
landscape so intently that he knew she must have
seen him. She was as trim and prim and dainty
as usual, sitting wedged in between her tiny withered
mother and a fat London tradesman. By-the-by,
Kitty's only fault was her way of addressing her
mother as "Mummy"; this was trying, for I never
saw any one so like a mummy as her mother.

Well, at last she condescended to look at Shane,
who was gazing on her hungrily; she greeted him
with her quiet smile and the shadow of a blush. His
heart sang raptures; her blush was the light of a sunset on snow, she was a spray of wood-anemone keeping dewy and dainty in the dusty thoroughfares of
life. This was the more ridiculous because she was
a prosy little creature; if he had told her she was a
spray of wood-anemone, she would have thought he
was mad.

Though he had come to Killarney to propose to
her, how was he to get a chance, even though her
mother was an ideal chaperon and carefully kept
out of the way? He might as well have left that to
Kitty, but I believe he thought her as innocent as a

babe, though she was singularly wide-awake. What with his raptures and his desperate efforts to invent some wily plan, he found the rest of the drive short. For all that, he had nearly emptied his pockets among the multitudinous beggars, before he reached the Gap of Dunloe, was grateful to them for taking the money, was in love with all the world.

When the party got down to walk through the Gap, Kitty greeted him in the calmest manner, giving him a hand like a small icicle. Then they walked down the narrow glen; on either side of it mountains prop the clouds, and a tiny bad-tempered river hurries through it, muttering and grumbling.

There was an old bald-headed eagle floating far up overhead near Purple Mountain; his only occupation is to sail round lazily, now and then, when he sees strangers coming, to make them think that Eagle's Nest Mountain is called after him. He looked down on the young couple with a kindly gleam in his eye, amused at the absurd contrast between Shane— big and swaggering, with a flush on his handsome face, and speaking fast with a mellow brogue, for he always has a brogue when he is excited—and pale Kitty Geraldine, with her quaint drawling accent. She was always hatefully cool. Sometimes the thought came to Shane that if he only dared seize her by the shoulders and shake her, it might do her a deal of good; but he dismissed the thought as a sacrilege.

That day she was even more perverse than usual; her American accent was more pronounced, her words more strange. She angered him by admiring his "cane"—as if he would be seen carrying a cane! Why, it was as healthy a bit of blackthorn as you could meet. She told him she had come from Dublin to Killarney on the "cars" in four hours; as if there was a car in Ireland that could travel at that rate. She told him she had seen Toole in London and that he was "lovely"; as if he did not know that Toole was anything but lovely.

Then when he flushed angrily, she glanced up at him with a look of child-like wonder in her grey eyes. So as Shane strode by her side he grew more and more indignant, and yet longed more and more to put his arms round her. Well they came to the end of the Gap, where the glen widens into Crom-Dhu, the Black Valley. The Valley is shut in by shadowy mountains, and the road winds round it, curving round a stretch of bog.

"Now, Mr. Desmond," said Kitty, "isn't this just like your old Europe? Why in Milwaukee we'd run a car right across the neck of this bog. What's more I'm going to set you an example; I'm going to take a short cut."

N

Then Shane was cruelly tempted; he knew what an Irish bog meant, and that a short cut through it was likely to prove a long journey, yet it would give him a chance to propose to Kitty. He tried to dissuade her, but it was with half his heart. She seemed demurely amused at something. It never dawned on him that she was giving him the chance he wanted.

"Then will you trust yourself to me?" he asked with a world of meaning in his voice.

"Why yes, of course," she said most innocently.

So they started on their short cut, leaving the rest of the sight-seers wondering. The old eagle —who still had an eye on them—chuckled and would have winked if he could. And the fat London tradesman, who was poetic and read Tupper, said this valley was an emblem of life, with its common and dull road lying between the bog and the mountains so that those who left it had either to climb a barren mountain till they were lost in the mists or to find a path for themselves across a quaking bog. For his part, he said, he preferred the prosy road, though in the long run it would bring him back very near where he started.

But his old wife, who was watching the couple— she must have had Irish blood in her, she had such a kind, jolly face—laughed and said that was all very well, but when they were a bit younger she would have walked through all the bogs in Ireland with him if he had said the word.

Then that bald-headed eagle—he hears everything —gave a scream of delighted laughter, for being Irish he loves honest sentiment, even when people are old and fat. "Tell me now," said a small lamb down by the lake-side, "tell me now, what's the matther wid that horrid old aigle? sure ye niver know whether he's laffin or in arnest."

Well, to cut a long story short, Shane and Kitty got across the bog somehow. He was in agony all the time lest she should wet the sole of her boot, so anxious about her that he trod in every pool of bog-water he came on. At the other side there was a brook running by the road. It was nothing to Shane, he strode across it; but when he looked back his heart stopped, for he saw that Kitty did not intend to risk wetting her small person. She stood still, looking even more demure than usual. To do him justice, he did not falter for a moment, though his heart was in his mouth. He stepped into the brook, splashing mightily; she drew back for fear a drop might touch her dainty grey dress. He took her in his arms; a new softness came to her eyes and a blush to her pale cheeks. He lifted her across, she was absurdly light.

The old eagle watched them with twinkling eyes. " 'Tis the first time that bit of a brook was anny use to annyone," he said to himself; then because he had the instincts of a gentleman, he turned his head away.

Shane felt it must be now or never.

"Kitty," he said—in a very low voice, with a tremble in it—" Kitty, if a fellow was to love you, worship you, though he knew he wasn't worthy to look at you, would there be any chance for him, Kitty ? "

"Why," she drawled innocently, "why that depends vurry much on who the fellow waws."

"Kitty," he said angrily, taking her by the shoulders, " Kitty, you little cruel child, how dare you treat me so? you'd infuriate a saint!" then suddenly with profound meekness—

"Ah, Kitty, dear heart! be kind to me! don't you know my heart is breaking for the love of yon? Kitty dear, will you be my wife ? "

"Why, yes," she said.

THE LEENAUN SHEE

"THESE many years," said the Rector, as he paced up and down his study—a snug room, though chilled by a raw light from the sea—"these many years, the books yonder have been my only companions; they are but a mean collection, some four hundred at most, yet they astound Clare. 'Is it possible, now,' said the Colonel to me, 'is it possible that you've read all those books?' But what would my life have been without them? With them I can forget my exile— in quiet weather, at least—but in winter this house rings with the hammering of the surf, and it is hard to read with a storm deafening you.

"This is a terrible place in winter; there is no peace from storms, and day after day there is a mist from the Atlantic, till those desolate moors and that irresolute line of hills become a welcome sight. Out of doors there are so few signs of life, that one is glad to see even a coracle overturned on the shingle and looking like a giant beetle. Then there is my enforced idleness. Why, man, at times I envy old Flannery his big troublesome congregation and his long night-rides to pray by some dying pauper.

    ‘ Wyd is his parische and houses fer asonder,’

but half my people are gentry who winter elsewhere. When I came here first I foresaw much leisure for writing ; but Moher took all the heart out of me. I scarcely know now whether to laugh or sigh thinking of the dreams I had when I was a pretty and precise boy at Oriel. Then only my certainty of future triumph made me bear life. Now I see that those were my shining days—

    ‘ Fulsere quondam candidi tibi soles.’

I wonder how many boys believe they have a great future before them. Faith, I would choose rather to have a great future behind me, and to look back on triumph. We begin with big hopes. ‘ Ainsi le bon temps regretons.’ Here,” he said opening a desk, ‘‘ here are the studies for my book, the book that died before it was born. I have written nothing now for a long time, yet you see no dust lies on them.

   ‘‘ Here is one I might read you, a study of Clarence Mangan for whom I have a great sympathy. If you find it faulty you must remember I was young when I wrote it.”

He sank into his easy arm-chair and began reading

with an obvious pleasure.   From the way he modulated his musical voice, you would have thought he
had a large audience.

" Long ago poets were romantic, they had flashing

" A NIGHT-RIDE "

eyes and flowing hair and a fine scorn of convention
and virtue.   Nowadays our writers of verse are fat
and jolly, and their looks are nearly as commonplace
as their books.   But the legends of Ireland say that

the old poets were loved by the Leenaun Shee. She haunted wild places, and the mortals she chose became strangers among men. When they saw her their eyes changed, and they abandoned the thoroughfares to follow her vainly. She made the pleasant ways of life hateful to them, but made them poets, and their songs shared her immortality.

"There is reason to believe that the Leenaun Shee has at length tired of love-making. It is a long time since she made her last choice, nearly ninety years. She chose a small Irish boy—James Mangan—he lived in a dirty back-street in Dublin, his father was poor and a grocer. And James Mangan to his dying day was cursed and blessed by her love; but the curse proved stronger than the blessing.

"He was then at a rough school, a nervous silent little wretch who shrank from his fellows, ridicule was agony to him: he was only happy when he could slink into a corner with a book, and at other times mooned and moped about uselessly; every one despised him. At home, too, he was miserable, his parents cared little for him, and I think he cared less for them: mind you, he was in no way a model. Then one morning, as he sat alone in the playroom, bent over some poetry-book, the 'Lay of the Last Minstrel' I think—the other boys were playing football out of doors in the mud, he could hear them

howling and yelling—suddenly the room filled with
light; he looked up and saw the Leenaun Shee.

" I, who have never seen her, cannot tell you what
she was like; but the boy's heart was made new as he
looked at her, he could not believe he had been
chosen for such happiness, would not have changed
his state with kings. This was his best moment, for
he never saw her again so clearly.

" The grocer failed; so the boy was put to support
the family, by working as an attorney's clerk. I
doubt whether he was of much use to the attorney.
Often as he sat copying out legal labyrinths of
words, that face came back to him, and his thoughts
wandered out of the dingy office to countries he was
never to know, shining islands and purple seas; then
he made absurd mistakes. Often he scribbled verses,
and very poor verses too, on the sly. It cheered him
to think that there was once an attorney's clerk,
Chatterton, who rose to be a poet and to poison himself. Now he blushed for his prosy name, so he
christened himself ' Clarence ; ' he felt sure that he
was a poet though in the world no one believed in
him. Well, after some years of this life, his health
broke down; he gave up his clerkship, and scraped a
livelihood, leading the easy and dignified life of a
bookseller's hack, writing in papers that have been
long forgotten. As he had a fragmentary scholar-

ship, a hazy knowledge of many languages, he wrote translations for bread. The Leenaun Shee haunted him, though he saw her seldom and dimly ; the one hope of his life was to win her.

"Then some young men set about founding a paper, *The Nation ;* they meant to change the world, they were dreamers who believed in the coming of freedom and truth and human brotherhood. Mangan joined them, wrote some admirable translations from Irish poets, and some strong verse of his own. The new paper woke Ireland to enthusiasm ; the young writers triumphed, they lectured O'Connell on politics and had serious thoughts of declaring war against England.

" But still the great poem that was to give Mangan his hope remained unwritten ; he made it in dreams and sometimes in his long lonely walks would rhyme to himself by the hour, but when he came to put pen to paper the inspiration was gone, so that he hated his writings. He aimed foolishly high, and could have earned money if he had been content to sing a slender song to fat sheep.

"By this time he affected singular clothes, ' a baggy pantaloon that was never intended for him, a short coat closely buttoned, a blue cloth coat still shorter, and a hat broad-leafed and steeple-shaped, the model of which he must have found in some picture of

Hudibras.' As he was small and lean, with a haggard face, wide blue eyes, and long golden hair, he was an ideal poet; and it is a pity we cannot force our writers of verse to dress in like fashion.

"This was a strange get-up for a man who shrank even from the eyes of his friends. He had suffered so much from the mockery of fools, that he now came to court it and to take pleasure in braving it. When he was a boy he would have died rather than have walked the streets of Dublin in such a dress.

"Though he shunned most of the young writers— their high spirits jarred on him, he was bitterly self-conscious, a man not easily understood, full of self-hatred and pride, friendly and solitary, longing for companionship and shrinking from companions—yet he made true friends among them. He was sadly out of place at rejoicings and usually sat silent, sometimes he broke in with forced attempts at jokes; life gave him small cause for laughing. One of his jokes speaks for itself. He said that the line in the *Faëry Queen* :

> 'The wretched man 'gan grinning horridlie'

was a misprint and should be read: 'The wretched Mangan grinning? horrid lie!'

"'For indeed,' said he, 'I think I shall never laugh again.'

" His new friends tried now to save him from himself; it was notorious that he drank.   He was always
ailing and downcast.   Happiness might have made
a new man of him; but he never had it, could only
get near it in drink.   Little drink was needed to
make him forget his failures and his follies, and see
himself as he wished he was.   Little drink was needed
to make him remember the face of the Leenaun Shee,
and forget his growing certainty that he would never
win her.   But he had no self-restraint, and his friends
saw this habit strengthening till it became a craving
he could not satisfy.

" Many called him mad, others looked down on him
for being such a poor shiftless creature, a few loved
him.   The worst of it was that he had only himself
to blame for his troubles.   People pointed out to him
that he might get on comfortably if only he had the
sense to be like every one else.

"Then he was given a place in the library of Trinity
College, and afterwards spent most of his time with
old books, his dearest companions because they knew
nothing of his weakness.   He felt that his friends
could not help looking down on him, or at least pitying
him, and he hated pity.   So daily he threw himself
more on the trusty companionship of the old writers,
friends who knew nothing of his failings, whose voices
spoke as kindly and as frankly to him as if he had

been saintly and wise, even if they had known him they were too great for contempt. Somebody describes him perched on the top of a step-ladder in a dark corner of the library, poring over a big folio. He had been always a book-worm, the dim library was his home; now he lived in a garret— no one knew where—so poor that he allowed none of his friends to see it. For some months he slept in a hayloft; but was turned out because he nearly set fire to the hay by reading at night. For weeks he would vanish; then he would come back looking even more haggard, wearing the same fantastic clothes in all weathers and all seasons, looking—as one of his friends said—'like the spectre of some German romance.'

"Things went from bad to worse with him. The triumph of *The Nation* passed; the young writers grew older and saw their dream fade into the light of common day: most of them reformed and became men of the world, some even rose to be successful politicians though they had once believed in freedom and truth. There is a story of Mangan quoting with tears in his eyes those lines of Ovid:

'Littora quot conchas, quot amœna rosaria flores,
    Quot-ve soporiferum grana papaver habet . . . .
        Tot premor adversis.'

"During these years, men had ground for calling

him mad. He spoke of constant horrible visions and seemed to confuse facts and dreams; set to work to write the history of his life, and produced a fiction with even less truth in it than most histories. A friend pointed out to him that much of it was untrue.

"'Well, then,' he answered, 'I must have dreamt it.'

"Then Dublin was struck by a plague of cholera. It came as a scourge to others, but it came as an angel to Clarence Mangan. The hospitals overflowed and sheds were built outside Dublin to hold the poorest cholera-stricken outcasts. He died in the pest-house. It is not known if the Leenaun Shee came to comfort her victim as he lay dying after so many miseries. But it seems likely that when she saw this end of his wasted life she repented of her flirting ways, knowing that it would have been better for him to have lived a grocer. If he had lived a grocer, he might have died a knight.

"This is why she takes no heed of latter-day writers of verse: she thinks they might do better as grocers. So, after all, Mangan's life was not useless, if it saved others from the curse of being poets.

"Trinity "—here the Rector folded his manuscript and made his voice even more musical, I think he knows all his writings by heart—"Trinity boasts

echoing names, but some think first there of the
man who was its servant and had no right to be
proud of its inheritance, find the Library haunted
by a stooping figure—with a white miserable face and
absurd clothes—and sacred to Clarence Mangan."

BISHOP O'HALLORAN

I KNEW a man once who had been a Bishop for a moment. His name was Garrett O'Halloran and he came from a village in Tipperary, Ballynaherloe I think it was called. He used to keep a shop in the Brompton Road near the Oratory; but it is closed and I have lost sight of him. He was a dealer in holy things; his shop was a little room so full of church ornaments and rare vestments that it seemed a sacristy, and its stock was doubled by a tall mirror at the far end. Often as I was going down the Brompton Road I turned into that outlandish shop, and I took a liking for O'Halloran who was a chirpy little fellow with frosty hair and a rosy bright face. He was mighty devout and spent half his spare time in the Oratory. His wares and his brogue delighted me, heartsick as I was of London and homesick for Ireland.

It was from his own lips that I had this story of his short eminence.

One day as he was leaning on his counter, waiting with more patience than hope for customers, a stranger came in, wearing the everyday dress of a Catholic Bishop; his presence was stately, and his manner had so gentle and tender a dignity that all good women and most dogs would have loved him at first sight. He had recently been named Bishop, he said—and spoke with such humility that O'Halloran could hardly believe him—Bishop of some infidel country; and he wanted an outfit of vestments and altar-vessels. A proud man was O'Halloran then; he brought out the treasures of his stock, crosiers and glittering mitres, mystical vestments—with long names that no layman is worthy to remember, even if he could—weighty rings, jewelled and golden chalices. The stranger was full of wonder. He was too lowly, he said, for such things : and yet what could be too glorious or too costly for the office that he had been forced to accept? He knew nothing of pomp and ceremony, his work had been among the poor; but would O'Halloran put on a mitre and vestments to show him how they looked? O'Halloran robed himself in the full pontificals of a Bishop; he put on wonderful vestments stiff with jewels and gold, leant his right

o

hand on a priceless crosier, and a mitre shone on his
head. Then as he saw himself so mirrored, for a
moment all the world changed to him. For that
moment he forgot his drudging and huckstering life,
he was no worried tradesman, but a brother of the
Apostles, and a bulwark of the Church. He forgot his
big ledgers and his daily task of smirking at chance
customers. Instead of the clatter of the Brompton
Road he heard the echo of Litanies; instead of his
shop he saw a Cathedral dimmed by incense and
crammed with worshippers, and he was the Shepherd
of that bowed multitude. For that moment he saw
all his common history become noble and beautiful;
and I, for one, have not the heart to blame him.
But he bought that fine moment at a great price:
for the stranger seized the two richest chalices, and
fled into the street. O'Halloran rushed to the shop-
door but even if a Bishop's robes had been better
suited for running he would not have hunted that
thief through Brompton with mitre and crosier for
all the Roman chalices. And the thief and the
chalices vanished down the Brompton Road.

"A LETTER FOR IRELAND"

I

As I was passing lately through Paradise Walk, I saw old Biddy Gallaher sitting on the doorstep of Johnson's house with her elbows on her knees and her dirty hands buried in her tousled grey hair. She seemed in high good humour and beamed on the world. But the world of that Chelsea slum took small heed of her smiles or her scowls; she was a depraved and lone old woman, her face was bloated, she was shaped like a tub, and her clothes were rags. There was no pause in her maundering talk except when she was asleep or drunk, and it took a power of whisky to silence her. Now she was holding forth eloquently, though a crippled baby sitting in the gutter near her was her only listener. The people of Paradise Walk were busy cheering two washerwomen who were fighting. Because the Connemara brogue was music to me, I stopped for a moment to hear Biddy.

"I'm me gran'mother," she was saying, "me own ould gran'mother dat did use to live in Ballinahadereen behind Leenaan on de road to Maam. She did use to sit so in de doorway, smokin' her black pipe, an' dere was no passin' her. An' me father, dacint man, God rest him! he couldn't get out of the house till she let him. He was terrible sthrong, but he'd rather have sthopped in there for iver, dan be rough wid de ould woman. 'Tis a pleasant place is Ballinahadereen an' de folk are kindly; dey bear wid ould women, and dey're gentle wid ye when ye're dhrunk, barrin' ye're fightin' dhrunk. Ah! 'tis dere I wish I was now. Dey do be tellin' me dat Ballinahadereen is de same as when I was a slip of a girl, wid de dung-heaps in front o' de houses, an' de sthrame runnin' down de middle of de sthreet, an' de blue shmoke comin' out of de chimney-holes in de tatch, an' de air smellin' of turf, an' de pigs, de craythurs, lookin' out of de front doors, an' de little pigs—de boneens—runnin' up de road afther ye, squealin' as if deir hearts was bruk. Dey do be sayin' dat 'tis de same—ah! but 'tis sore and hard to believe it. I was a good girl when I was dere; surely dat was ages and ages ago afore de mountains was made. When I was a colleen wid a shawl over me head, I did use to walk to Mass at Leenaan, four miles ivery morn, snow or shine, pickin' me way 'long de road to keep clare of de puddles an' de sthones. Often den I was barefooted; now I've boots, gran' boots, if dey weren't burst an' me toes weren't stickin' out of

"GOING TO MASS"

dem. Dat was afore I married me man—ould Mick —God rest his poor soul! afore Mick came to London to make his fortune, bad luck to him! ' In London,' says Mick to me, ' in London, I do be hearin' all the world's rich, why, de poor dere are rich.' "

Here Johnson the cabman appeared suddenly behind Biddy; there was not room for him to pass out. "Get out of the way; you old drunken fool," he said.

"I'm me ould gran'mother," answered Biddy, "dis is Ballinabadereen; no one shall pass barrin' I let dem."

Johnson flung her off the doorstep; she fell forward on her head and lay stunned on the footpath. In a moment there was a crowd round us; I suppose the fight was finished. The people were delighted with Johnson's humorous act; but the crippled baby squalled, probably it had good cause to feel for the victims of rough treatment. Then an old man tried to lift Biddy. Seeing that no one would give him a hand, I helped to carry her upstairs. I repented it, for she was very heavy and her clothes were greasy and filthy.

II

About a week later, I was going down the Queen's Road towards Cheyne Walk. It was chill foggy weather and the slush was thick in the streets. The lamps had been just lit and were gilding the puddles, and I could see a row of lights diminishing along the misty Embankment.

As I passed the mouth of Paradise Walk I saw a crowd. They were badgering and baiting an old

woman; she was drunk I supposed. Then I saw it
was old Biddy Gallaher, and for once she looked sober.
But her conduct was singular, she was walking side-
ways up the slum with her arms out straight.

"I'm a crab," she was saying, "I'm a crab, an'
I'm walkin' in an' out o' de yellow seaweed dat hangs
on de rocks by Leenaan."

The crowd roared with delight. "Wot a game!"
they said, "she's off her nut and she thinks she's a
crab." They were making way for her to pass.
Time was when she could have made way for herself
and have cleft a path through the thickest mob like
a tornado.

Suddenly she turned on them raging. "How dar
ye follow me here, ye crule bastes?" she yelled.
"Dis isn't London—isn't dis Ireland, how dar ye
come here?" Here she cursed the crowd with
incredibly vile language; and the more eloquent
she grew, the more they enjoyed it.

Then as she reached the mouth of the slum and
saw the red pillar-box in Queen's Road before her,
"No! I'm not a crab," she cried. "I'm a letther for
Ballinahadereen. For a penny sthamp I can go all
de way dere." She butted her tousled head against
the slit of the box. "I can't get in," she said, "ah!
put me in! or I'll be late for de post."

Policeman 309 J, whose name in private life is

Patrick McFadden, came swaggering towards her.
" Move on there now," he said.

" Is it move on, consthable ? Isn't that what I'm
wantin' to do ? I'm a letther for Ireland. If I was
an ould woman now, I'd niver see me home more.
But I'm a letther, and for a penny sthamp I'm goin'
sthraight all de way to Ballinahadereen on de road to
Maam. For de dear God's sake give me a sthamp,
consthable."

" A stamp ? 'tis a shove I'll be givin' ye," said
Policeman 309 J. " Move on now, good woman, or
I'll be after running you in." But Biddy went on
butting the pillar and crying that it was a disgrace
to a Christian country to make the letter-boxes so
small. " Come on then," said the policeman, kindly
enough, " Come on then, it's the General Post Office
I'll be taking you to." He went off with Biddy
hanging on his arm lovingly.

And now I hear that Biddy is to be found in
Bethlehem Hospital. She must look odd since she
is forced to dress neatly. She keeps a dirty black
stamp stuck over her left eyebrow, and they say
would rather die than have it washed off. " I'm a
letther for Ireland," she cries to every one. " Post
me quick or I'll be late for de mail. Ah ! for de
dear God's sake, post me quick, dat I may be goin' to
Ballinahadereen on de road to Maam."

CONSTABLE COYNE

A WHITE cottage with barred windows faces Father
Flannery's chapel just outside Moher Village, on the
Liscannor Road. When first I saw it, I wondered
at its cleanliness; and then Shane Desmond told me
that it was the headquarters of order in Moher—the
Constabulary Barracks. At most times its rank is
plain, for you can see stalwart and stately constables
lounging in the doorway. Nowadays they have a
quiet life because Moher is quiet. You meet them
lounging affably through the Village, or patrolling
the roads with a leisurely dignity. The folk greet
them cheerily; and the girls make eyes at them as
they pass by. Moher is quiet because Shane Desmond is worshipped. His wife brought him so many
dollars that he need trouble no one for rent. He is
so lenient and kind now, that he is often cited as a
model to landlords who are desperately struggling to
make both ends meet. But in the old days when
Shane was poor and at daggers-drawn with his

tenants and used to ride through his own fields
armed to the teeth, the constables had a different
experience. Seeing them then, you would have
thought they were the outposts of an invader. In
those days every man's hand was against them, and

"GUARDING MOONLIGHTERS"

they risked their lives, loyally helping to quell their
own country and to punish the crimes of their kindred. Often when I saw them stoically guarding
Moonlighters, paying no heed to the curses of the
crowd following them, or patrolling the Liscannor
Road after dark with rifles and bayonets, and looking
over the low walls every now and then to make sure

that their nearest relations were not lying in ambush, I found it hard to believe that they had been bare-footed boys in Irish villages and reared under thatched roofs.

One of the men quartered in Moher is a friend of mine, Constable Martin Coyne. I got to know him when he was one of Shane's body-guard. He is a stiff soldierly man with a long grey moustache and cropped hair, a very quiet and methodical fellow. I made friends with him because I found that he has a great stock of stories and a deal of dry humour.

He is nearly as learned in legends as Colonel Hercules Desmond, but tells them with a prosy simplicity that makes them easy to believe, while the Colonel's are sometimes so eloquent that one is tempted to think him a man of less truth than tongue. Some day I shall mould the Colonel's traditions of the old riotous times and the constable's grim stories of the Moonlighters and the " Mountainy Men " into a book telling of Lord Theobald Butler's last duel and of the burning of Davernmore and of the hanging of Sir Bartholomew Blake, showing how the White-boys beleaguered Crowe Castle in the dead of a winter's night when there was thick snow on the ground, how ' John-o'-the-Blanket ' (who was so named because he divided his life between his bed

and his saddle) hunted the 'Peep-o'-day Boys,' and
how the Devil hunted 'John-o'-the-Blanket.'

Here is one of the constable's stories—how Sergeant Molloy, who was shot afterwards at an eviction
near Lahinch, climbed the Devil's Mother Mountain
by night with a dozen constables to capture a Still.

Constable Coyne during the first years of his
service, was quartered at Leenane in Connemara
under Sergeant Molloy. The times were troubled,
and the constables had plenty to do, quieting the
turbulent Joyces. Sergeant Molloy, though a man
of an easy and jolly temper, was a keen worker;
though he loved a cheery fireside, he spent night
after night patrolling the mountain roads in the
maddest weather; though he was a fine judge of
"potheen," he was unrelenting in his search for illicit
Stills. There was a Still high up on the Devil's
Mother Mountain that was an eyesore and a misery
to him. The whole countryside knew its whereabouts;
for by day its blue curl of smoke could be seen from
the highroad and by night its fire shone like a star
on the dim summit. But a keen look-out was kept;
and when the constables climbed the Mountain they
found only a wilderness of rocks. Many a night
Sergeant Molloy shook his fist at that star. So when
at last an informer, Silent Mick Mulcahy—one of the

Mountainy Men, a shepherd who lived alone on the Blue Gable Mountain and rarely set foot in the valleys—came stealthily and offered to guide the constable by an unguarded path to the Still, the sergeant received him with open arms, sent post-haste to summon help, and set out after dusk.

Silent Mick was a man of sad countenance and of exceedingly few words. His silence seemed to damp the spirits of the party, though they needed little damping, for it was black boisterous weather, and no one but the sergeant had the least wish to climb the Devil's Mother in the darkness, to have a midnight struggle with the Mountainy Men. The constables were armed to the teeth, for the men aloft were desperate and lawless.

At the Old Hag's Glen, four men from Carrala joined them ; then they began to climb the Mountain. The light above seemed brighter than usual, as big as a carriage lamp. It was rough climbing, for Silent Mick took them by an incredible path, over slippery rocks and up cliffs ; he led them plodding through boggy glens and wading up flooded streams. It was pitch dark, and Molloy had forbidden them to use their lanterns. The night was uncanny; the wind was hooting and wailing, and strange lights sparkled on the summit. All Connemara knows that to see wandering and mysterious lights on the mountain-tops is an omen of death. It seemed to them that they were hours and hours clambering and floundering; sometimes the path seemed downhill. "My word," said Molloy, "'tis no wonder this path isn't guarded." He had more than half a mind to turn back and take Silent Mick with him in hand-cuffs; when suddenly he heard an echo of singing from overhead. "Ay," said Mick, "'tis mighty merry they do be up yonther, so it is. Mebbe they'll be quiether when we're bringin' them down."

Sometimes the singing was clear, echoing strangely from the rocks, sometimes the wind drowned it, and sometimes it was like the singing of ghosts. The songs changed; one voice would lead faintly, and then would come an echoing chorus and the music of a fiddle and bag-pipe. "Sure enough," said Mick "'tis a great dance they're havin'."

"Faith, there's an army of them up there," said the sergeant.

At last, just as they could see a frosty glimmer of moon-rise through the scudding clouds, the wind fell for a moment, and the singing rang out so near them that they could hear the words of the song, it was "Och! Johnny, I hardly knew ye!" They gathered closer and hurried on with a fresh heart, forgetting that they were dripping, footsore and bruised. By the redness of the mists above they knew that a big fire must be burning. Then as they were wading, ankle-deep in a stiff stream, through a black gorge—a gash in the mountain—suddenly at a turn they came in sight of their prey.

Right before them on a ledge of rock, some hundred yards higher, a huge bonfire blazed in front of a cave, with great scrolls of flame waving in the wind. Round it a ring of men and women were jigging, and the blaze half showed a throng behind them —some squatting on the rocks, some standing— and shone on the barrels of rifles and revolvers, and on the curling "worm" of the Still. At that moment, the throng caught up the yell, "Hurroo! Hurroo!" and then the chorus:

> "Wid dhrums an' guns an' guns an' dhrums
> Th' inimy nearly shlew ye,
> Me darlin' dear, ye look so queer!
> Och! Johnny, I hardly knew ye!"

For a minute the climbers stood breathless. "Upon me soul!" said the sergeant, "this is no joke! Sure they've got the whole counthryside together. What d'ye think of it, consthable?"

"I think," said Constable Coyne, "that Leenane is a mighty pleasant place."

"But sure they wouldn't know how manny we are. Couldn't we be after surprisin' them, Mulcahy?"

But Silent Mick Mulcahy had vanished. Next moment they heard a whoop from the darkness behind them. Instantly the singing and dancing stopped. The revellers up above fell back on either side of the fire, so that there was no knowing their faces. One man—a big fellow in knee-breeches and a long coat—came to the front of the ledge and peered down into the gorge. He had a rifle, and his black figure looked gigantic against the flames behind him, " upon a background of pale gold."

" Ah, an' is that you Sergeant Molloy, me jewel ? " said he. " We take it mighty kind o' ye to be comin' all the way up here to our dancin'; an' 'tis a terrible wild night, so it is! Ah, hurry up the cliff now, man, an' have a bit an' a sup. I've a dhrop here for ye that 'll drive the cold from your heart ; 'twill so, an' you such a great judge of potheen."

But the sergeant was in no mood for joking. " Come down o' that now, ye foolish ass," he shouted, " or I'll make ye."

There was a great shout of laughing from the crowd by the fire ; it echoed from the cave and the rocks.

" Ah, Sergeant," the man went on—and he seemed grieved—" I take shame o' your manners. If you'd offered me a dhrop, would I have answered ye so ? An' there's poor Mick Mulcahy, that we sent all the way to Leenaue t' invite ye to the dance. Hasn't he

"UPON A BACKGROUND OF PALE GOLD"

been sthravagin' up and down the Mountain wid ye for hours, afeard ye'd be here too soon?"

"Ye may well call him poor Mick if I get hould of him," cried the sergeant.

Again there was a roar of laughing, and a shout, "Long life to ye, Silent Mick! Your soul man!"

"Ah, sergeant dear," cried the man on the ledge, "is that an example to be settin', an' you wid all your young men wid ye? What'll Martin Coyne be thinkin' of ye? Are ye there, Consthable Coyne?"

"I am here," shouted Constable Coyne, "an' by the powers I'll make ye wish I wasn't!"

With that he rushed forward and came on a straight cliff under the ledge. The constables opened their dark lanterns only to find themselves trapped in a black gorge with unclimbable walls. Up above, the revellers crowded to the front of the ledge, laughing and whooping till every echo in the Mountain answered.

The constables were shown now by the light of the lanterns; and the crowd recognising them, howled at them and taunted them each.

"Ah, be aisy, Johnny Molloy," shouted the big man above, "ye'll be hurtin' yourself if ye're so wild. Tell me now, are ye listenin' to me? Don't ye know the way home? Sure ye've only to walk sthraight down the middle o' that little sthrame."

But Sergeant Molloy though naturally a merry and easy man, was now choking with rage. He fired at the humourist. The crowd huddled back into the darkness, and there was a fusillade of echoes. The big man had not moved. "'Pon me soul, this is too bad o' ye, Sergeant. This is a black night for Ireland! Ah! but they'll be glad to hear this in England. That an Irishman should fire at another for offering him a dhrink. Tell me now, are ye listenin' to me? If ye don't go home out of that this minit, we'll dhrown ye wid rocks."

He turned and said something in Irish to the crowd. They answered with a shout of laughing; plainly the whole thing was the greatest of jokes to them. Many of them ran forward and lit torches at the fire; then they all scattered into the darkness on either side of the gorge.

The constables were huddled in consultation. They could see no one, but the great bonfire was towering, and along the cliffs on either hand was the light of torches.

"They'll not be believin' me, boys!" shouted the leader from somewhere on the left cliff. "Give them a few dhrops o' rocks!"

"And then," said Constable Coyne, when he told me the story, "then wid a howl that ye'd have heard at Leenane, they began rollin' rocks on us; the air was chokin' wid them. We didn't wait long. In a minit and a half we were going down the Mountain annyhow. It's my belief that every soul for miles round was on the Mountain that night, whoopin' an' hurrooshin' an' singin' an' brandishin' their torches.

"An' next day all the folk we met looked as innocent as lambs. But 'twould have taken a brave man to name the Devil's Mother Mountain to the sergeant. And manny a long hour he spent lookin' for Silent Mick Mulcahy."

EPILOGUE

TREASURE-TROVE

"In sleep a King; but waking no such matter."

LAST night as I sat here alone I had a queer dream. Hours spent reading at the Museum had given me the right head-ache, and for once I was sick of books. There was a fog out-of-doors, and my chambers were dimmed by it. It must have been late, for I remember noticing the growth of the noises from Fleet Street. In my quiet court I can hear nothing of the traffic in the daytime, but in the stiller hours of the night the clatter of hoofs on the wood pavement echoes through the outlying parts of the Temple. Keeping awake needed an effort, and I dozed with a fat book open before me.

Suddenly I heard a cheery voice. I started and rubbed my eyes. In the arm-chair on the other side of my cramped fireplace sat Colonel Hercules Desmond. His open-air voice sounded very loud in my hushed chambers. What could have brought him all this long way from the wilds of Liscannor? He wore his old shooting-coat and muddy gaiters—strange clothes to wear on so long a journey. At the sight of him I could have sworn that the fog in my room was a mist from the Atlantic, and that the musty air had a tang of the sea.

"Upon my word!" he was saying, "that Madden's a wonderful man. All my life I've been worried for money; and now Madden, he finds a coal-mine there in my park, and bog-oak in Liscannor bog, and begad, I'm the richest man in County Clare. The old days shall come again now. I'll build a house bigger than Castle Desmond, and plant half the county with trees; I'll have open house all the year round and only gentlemen shall set foot in it, none of your swindling businessmen. And I'll have the happiest tenantry in Ireland, but not one of them shall drink tea; it's the curse of Ireland the way the peasants drink tea now, it makes rickety old women of them, they shall drink whisky like men. And if any one on my estates dares give me a cross look I'll evict him on the spot."

"I always knew 'twas there." The jolly voice had changed into a slow melancholy brogue; instead of the Colonel I saw McCaura, the Moonlighter. "I always knew 'twas there, the dimon' mine in th' acre. Manny's the time when I turned up pebbles wid me spade I thought I'd found't, and when at last that wet evenin'—sore I was from the long sthoopin', wid an empty belly an' a sick heart—there was the pebble on the lump, but for the wet I'd niver 've seen the shine of't, an' 'twas no pebble but a dimon'. An' now I'll marry Miss Aileen, she'll 've iverythin' in the world, jules an' a queen's carridges an' the height o' good livin'; an' ivery soul in Moher 'll live rent-free wid nothin' to do an' wid lashin's o' dhrink; an' I'll be a fine gintleman wid gran' horses o' me own, an' 'll rune the Shnipe, I'll be the death o' the Shnipe afther all."

"Is that a fact now?" In place of McCaura I saw the Snipe himself, with his long legs stretching across my worn hearthrug. "Is that a fact, now? But I can tell you, sir, when I got that American letter saying my uncle was dead and I rich, but I was glad of it. For I'm sick of being shot at; I'm a quiet man by nature. And I'm sick of doing the landlords' work, taking the blame while they take the money. And it's a great thing for my boy; he'll settle down now. It's easy for a rich man to keep out of trouble; it's the poor who are always in scrapes. And Jane, my wife, she'll be changed, too, she'll be

like she was when she was young; poor girl, she's
had a hard time making ends meet. Ah! poverty's
a cruel thing for one's temper."

"Mebbe ye've heard tell," the voice was now shrill
and whining. It was Dark Andy, the little blind
beggarman, that I saw before me. His big coat was
more ragged than ever; his shock of grey hair was
as rough as if it had just been tousled by the wind on
the Cliffs of Moher. "I wonder," I said to myself,
"how on earth he found his way here; surely they'd
mob him in the streets. And I hope that dirty old
coat of his won't be ruining my arm-chair, faith, it's
bad enough already."

"Mebbe," he said, "ye've heard tell of the Leprechaun, the tiny ould craythur that spends all his
time mendin' an ould shoe. He'll have nought to say
to the rest of the Little Good People, but sits all alone
hammerin' at the ould shoe an' can niver finish it.
Terrible rich he is; crocks full of gold and a power
of threasure he has hidden. That's why he's lone,
afeard they'd be chatin' him out of it, so it is. If ye
can catch hould of him and keep your eye on him,
he'll have to fill your pockets wid gold. But take
your eye off him an' he's gone like the dew in the
mornin'. Manny's the time I've heard him hammerin'
at the shoe at the Liscannor Crossroads an' he sittin'

high up in the branches. 'Ah,' says I to meself, ' if only I could grip hould of him, I'd niver let on that I'm dark. Surely I'd get the threasure.' An' manny's the time he's wished me a good mornin'; he'd the weeniest voice, it sounded as if 'twas miles away, so it did. But I niver let on that I heard him. An' yestherday morn—gran' rough weather 'twas an' the wind yellin'—the Leprechaun he calls out from right over me, ' the top o' the mornin' to ye, Misther Lonergan.' An' I niver heeded him. Then afther a minit says he louder, 'Good mornin', Misther Lonergan,' an' I went on playin' me fiddle. Then agin I heard him, an' oh me soul! how me heart jumped! for I knew by his voice he'd clambered down the tree an' was a-sittin' on the root next me. ' Is it deaf y'are as well as dark, sir?' says he—mighty fretful an' peevish, ' D'ye call it manners niver to be passin' me the time o' day or givin' me a good morrow an' I workin' by ye so often ? ' I laid me fiddle down out o' the way. I thrembled as if I was dyin'. I turns sharp on the Leprechaun an' I clutches him in me arms—ah ! the happiness o' that moment ! ' I'm a made man,' thinks I, ' I've the threasure at last.'

" ' I have me eye on ye,' I screeches.

" ' Let me go this minit, y' ould idjit, or I'll be hittin' ye,' says he. ' How can ye have your eye on me an' you dark ? '

" ' I'm not dark,' says I, ' I've been foolin' ye all the time to git hould of ye.'

" ' What ! ' he screeches, an' begins to sthruggle an' fight like a divil—my soul ! but the little craythur was sthrong ! Twas like houldin' a weasel barrin' the bites ; but I clutched him like 'twas life I was grippin'. Soon the breath was out of him an' he lies quiet against me, gaspin' like a fish that ye've just caught.

" ' Is it dark I am ? ' says I, ' sure that's easy disproved. What's there that I can't see ? That's a mighty fine fern growin' out of the wall yonther ' (I'd felt it often) ' and them nettles by it, they are terrible tall ' (didn't I know it well, bad luck to them !). ' That's a great hotel they're buildin' over yonther at Lisdoonvarna ' (hadn't I heard of it ?) ' an' the roof lies off poor Jim O'Brien's house over there by Lahinch ' (didn't I know he'd been evicted ?) ' an' the clothes ye're wearin' they're a green coat, red kneebreeches an' brown sthockins' (sure all Ireland knows what the Leprechaun wears) ' an' that's a terrrible handsome coat ye have sir ! '

" ' An' that's thrue ivery word of it ! ' says he, ' upon me life, ye're a great man ! To be foolin' all Ireland these manny years ! I'm proud to know ye, Misther Lonergan. I'll be givin' you lashin's of gold in the twinklin' of an eye.'

"I let go of him, he jumps to the other side of me, but I heard him: 'twas like a bird hoppin' on a twig. I turns to him, 'Be aisy there, I have me eye on ye,' I says. I hear him rummagin' by the trees. He comes back.

" 'Here's an armful o' threasure, it's gold, don't ye see it is?'

" ' 'Tis so,' says I, but I thinks, mebbe 'tis what they call gold but it feels mighty like wilthed cowslips. 'So I've got the threasure,' says I to meself, 'an' faith, now I wonther what I wanted it for. What's the use of all the threasure of all the world to me an' I dark?'

" 'Then,' says the Leprechaun, wheedlin'-like, 'An' now, Misther Lonergan, I've a power o' respect for ye. 'Tisn't often I meet a man that can get the betther of me. So what else can I do for ye? Say but the word.' An' what is there that the Little Good People can't do? All at once I disremembers he was foolin' me.

" 'Ah, sir!' I says, 'for the sake o' the merciful God that made both of us, give the light to me! Give me back me eyes!'

"The Leprechaun he flames wid rage. 'Y'ould benighted fool!' he screeches, 'didn't I tell ye y'are dark? To think that a dark man should be afther putthin' the comether on me so! Isn't it bad enough to have half the men in Ireland huntin' for me, to git hould o' me threasure? Sure if all the dark men that beg by the waysides take to lookin' out for me how can I iver get this blessed ould shoe finished by the Day of Judgment?' An' wid that he was gone, an' I buried the threasure unther the roots o' the trees."

" 'Tis wonderful, me dear, what things you can do with money."

Why, it was Peter Flannery.

"Ah, now, is that you, Father Peter?" I said. I had no idea I should be so glad to see his grim face. There is an absurd boyishness about him that makes me feel young, too. Often I have found myself talking to him in my wildest forgotten brogue, just as if I was still an ugly little Irish boy with the world before me, and not cursed with foresight.

" 'Tis wonderful, me dear. All me life I've been poor, never knowing when I wouldn't have a penny, and glad to have annything; for if ye'd expected to go to Hell ye'd think Purgatory was Paradise. An manny's the time when I was a boy at Ballyvaughan that I dreamt of findin' the big Spanish ships that were lost off Spanish Point. But is there a fisherman annywhere round that hasn't that dream? Hundreds and hundreds of years ago they were lost

an' they chokin' with gold an' all this time they
rotted under the sea. An' now I've foun' them an' I
never would 've foun' them but that I was comin'
back from Caherrush in Lonergan's ould hooker from
buryin' Kitty O'Brien that was me sister's child,
God rest her! 'Twas a still day and the boat scarce
moved; and far down I saw the ship like a shadow
lyin' on a ledge of rock. An' now that I've lashin's
of money Pathrick shall 've new clothes (the little
omadhaun! he'd wear out a suit of armour in a week)
an' the best of eddication, an' Mary Shaughnessy,
me housekeeper, she'll 've a real silk dress, an'
there's manny a poor soul in this counthry-side shall
laugh with joy, an' I'll build a cathaydral in Moher.
What's that ye say, me dear? Isn't Moher small
for a cathaydral? I know, I know, but aren't half the
cathaydrals in Ireland built in places no bigger?"

Suddenly Peter's slow tones changed to a musical
modulated voice.

"There was a singular fitness," said the Rector,
"a singular fitness in my finding the treasure those
old benighted monks buried in Liscannor bog when
Cromwell hunted them. And who else in Clare
could make such good use of it? For now I shall
leave Moher and buy a house somewhere near Oxford
—a little house with an old park round it and with

glimpses of the spires through the trees—and make it homely with many books and comely with pictures. When I was young I was hopeful; but here my mind's life has been robbed of its manhood. I can say of it in Fletcher's phrase :

> ' 'Tis not a life
> 'Tis but a piece of childhood thrown away.'

The city Kilsafeen lies drowned by the shore of Arran : flags of seaweed float from the roofs of its palaces. But when Ireland grows happy, Kilsafeen shall rise and the fish shall forget it. So my drowned hopes are rising; who knows but I may write my book after all ? "

Then my dream changed. I was alone, still in my musty room, but gladness had come to me.

"Now," I said, "now that I've found my amazing treasure—a pleased public and a virtuous publisher—I'll charter a yacht and load it with a cargo of books and some dozen friends—old Jones shall be there and young Smith and middle-aged Robinson, women, too, some of them old in the world's eyes, but every one on board (even the cabin-boy) must be young in heart—and Aileen shall be the hostess. We shall haunt the warm waters, and linger among the palm-islands.   We shall sail coasting where the mountains look on Marathon."

" Is Lady Davern at home ? "
Somehow I was at a hall-door in Merrion Square.
" Lady Davern is it ?   She is, sir," answered the honeyed butler.
Could that be Aileen—that mature, worldly matron ?   And was that tiny Davern her Treasure-trove ?

Printed by BALLANTYNE, HANSON AND CO.
London and Edinburgh.

CPSIA information can be obtained at www.ICGtesting.com
Printed in the USA
LVOW122110070612

285194LV00003B/209/P

9 781143 957116